HEART OF MISSISSIPPI

Hot sultry nights with delicious docs—
in the heart of Mississippi...

Kelsey and China Davis grew up with dark secrets
that rocked their once steady family foundations.
While China wants to stay in Golden Shores,
Kelsey can't wait to leave...

But neither sister expects to meet the two
gorgeous docs who have come to Golden Shores
searching for a fresh start. And once the fireworks
begin it's not long before pulses are racing and
temperatures are rising!

The second story in Susan Carlisle's
***Heart of Mississippi* duet**

THE MAVERICK WHO RULED HER HEART

is also available this month
from Mills & Boon® Medical Romance™

Dear Reader

For many years I've spent a week here and a week there on the Gulf Coast. I've been to a number of places in the world, but the beaches of the Gulf are the most beautiful. Clean white sand, radiant sunshine, friendly people—pure pleasure. When I placed China and Payton in this setting I knew it would be a wonderful backdrop for their romance. Their love story has been great fun to write. No two people could be more different and more alike at the same time. It was joy mixed with frustration trying to get China and Payton together while they were fighting to stay apart.

On a personal note, my heart goes out to anyone who has been touched by cancer. My family and friends certainly have been. I look forward to the day when this ugly disease is eradicated for ever. I'd also like to add a special thank-you for the quality help I received from the staff of the Crestview Nursery in Crestview, Florida. All the plant information was much appreciated. I love you all.

I hope you enjoy Payton and China's story. I like to hear from my readers. You can find me at www.SusanCarlisle.com

Susan

THE DOCTOR WHO MADE HER LOVE AGAIN

BY
SUSAN CARLISLE

First published in Great Britain 2014
by Mills & Boon, an imprint of Harlequin (UK) Limited,
Eton House, 18-24 Paradise Road, Richmond, Surrey, TW9 1SR

© 2014 Susan Carlisle

ISBN: 978-0-263-24392-5

... that are natural,
grown in
sses conform
rigin.

Susan Carlisle's love affair with books began when she made a bad grade in maths in the sixth grade. Not allowed to watch TV until she'd brought the grade up, she filled her time with books and became a voracious romance reader. She has 'keepers' on the shelf to prove it. Because she loved the genre so much she decided to try her hand at creating her own romantic worlds. She still loves a good happily-ever-after story.

When not writing Susan doubles as a high school substitute teacher, which she has been doing for sixteen years. Susan lives in Georgia with her husband of twenty-eight years and has four grown children. She loves castles, travelling, cross-stitching, hats, James Bond and hearing from her readers.

Recent titles by Susan Carlisle:

SNOWBOUND WITH DR DELECTABLE
NYC ANGELS: THE WALLFLOWER'S SECRET*
HOT-SHOT DOC COMES TO TOWN
THE NURSE HE SHOULDN'T NOTICE
HEART SURGEON, HERO...HUSBAND?

NYC Angels

**Also available in eBook format
from www.millsandboon.co.uk**

Dedication

To Zach
I love you, Z.

Praise for
Susan Carlisle:

'Susan Carlisle pens her romances beautifully…
HOT-SHOT DOC COMES TO TOWN is a book that I
would recommend not only to Medical Romance fans but
to anyone looking to curl up with an angst-free romance
about taking chances and following your heart.'
—*HarlequinJunkie.com* on
HOT-SHOT DOC COMES TO TOWN

CHAPTER ONE

WHAT WAS THIS guy doing? China Davis waited for the driver to park so she could take the space next to him. She watched appalled as the red-hot-off-the-line foreign sports car straddled the parking line.

Really? This person was going to take up two spaces in the far-too-small parking lot during morning rush hour?

Disgusted, China observed the driver do just as she'd feared. She would have to go around the building and park in the strip mall parking lot. She'd be lucky if she could juggle the donuts and coffee back to the car without spilling one or both all over her scrubs.

China glanced at the tag on the slick vehicle as she passed. Illinois. It was a little early for the summer crowd to be showing up. Still mid-May, she'd been looking forward to another few weeks of peace before the beach mob invaded.

Living in a small southern coastal town had its advantages but there was a downside also. Four out of the twelve months the locals had to contend with the influx of people. It didn't help that here was only one main road into town, which had no choice but to end when it met the water of the gulf. From there the driver had to choose east or west along the beach.

Dolly's Donuts was located on the main road. As the

local morning hangout for the senior citizens, it was also the place in town for quality donuts. China's mom had pointed out more than once to her that patience was a virtue. That might be so but China had promised hot donuts, and she didn't like to disappoint.

As she hurried into Dolly's, she mentally reviewed her order list. She glanced at her wrist watch. Yes, she was going to be late. Something that had never happened before. The line at the counter was four deep when she slipped into the tight glassed-in space that was Dolly's customer area. The place still had the feel of a fifties-era coffee shop, with a few metal stools with orange seats facing a long narrow counter.

China studied the tall man in front of her with the wide shoulders. His dark hair was cut supershort, as if it had been shaved off and was beginning to grow out.

One customer down, three more to go.

Her attention returned to the man. He wore a salmon-color polo shirt that fit him loosely but contrasted nicely with his dark coloring.

She peeked around him to see what was happening with the next patron. The man gave her a pointed look and she straightened, finding her place in line again. Her father had used that same look to make her and her siblings fall in line.

Another down. China stepped forward. Thankfully the man ahead of her was next.

"What do you consider your best donut?" he asked.

Oh, no! He was going to get Roger started on donuts. She'd be lucky to make work by lunchtime.

Dolly's husband stated in a voice of authority from behind the cash register, "We sell a lot of these." He pointed to a tray of glazed. "But the best, I believe, are the double chocolate. We make a special…"

China zoned out as Roger went into a monologue on how the dough was prepared.

"I'll get you some fresh ones from the back."

"That sounds great," the man in front of her said, as if he had all the time in the world. He probably did, but she sure didn't. They were expecting her at the clinic and she needed to be on time. She worked hard not to receive complaints about her actions; she wanted no conflict.

When Roger ambled off, China leaned around the man and said in a low voice, "You're not from around here or you'd know better. Don't ever get Roger started. It goes on forever."

The man pinned her with a dark look of disapproval that made her chest tighten as she shrank back into her place. He turned his back to her again. She wouldn't be saying anything further to this guy.

In the brief moment she'd seen his face straight on she'd been able to tell he was thin. No tan line marked his temple from eye to ear where sunglasses might have been. In fact, he looked as if he could use a little time outside. Still, he had an interesting face. Not handsome in the Hollywood leading man sense of the words but more in an attention-grabbing way.

"Here you go," Roger said. "How about coffee?"

"Black," the man said in one deep syllable.

Roger turned away and a full minute later slid the coffee container across the counter and quoted the man his total.

With relief, China moved closer, anticipating her turn. As she did so the man rotated and bumped against her.

"Excuse me," he said, with an air of authority.

"I'm sorry," China said, sliding to the side to dodge his coffee cup and moving well out of his way. She didn't want to cause any more of a scene. It had been on impulse for her to have spoken to him to begin with.

He strolled by her before she turned to placed her order. While Roger bagged it she looked out the glass doors at the broad back of the exasperating man. He headed straight for the fancy sports car. *I should have known.*

The man was one of those who thought he was entitled because he was handsome and drove a fancy car!

Payton pulled the Mercedes into a parking space behind the clinic to face a wall of greenery that was overgrown. In his other life it would have been another row of cars in a spiraling parking garage. He looked at the 1940s wooden house that had been converted into a treatment center. The Golden Shores Walk-in Clinic in Mississippi. It was nothing like the state-of-the-art facility he was used to, nothing resembling the highly charged ER in Chicago where ambulance sirens blared every few minutes.

Truthfully, nothing about Golden Shores was like the place he'd called home his entire life. Here the buildings went no higher than three levels when he was used to skyscrapers and glittering glass. Two-lane roads were the norm. None of those eight-lane interstates with cars whizzing by. If he got behind a truck pulling a boat then he had to sit back for the ride. Everything moved slower and people spoke with a drawl. But this was what he wanted. The easier pace, the chance to enjoy life. A place to recover. He'd moved nine hundred miles from family and friends to find his own destiny. Cancer had taken its toll and now it was time for him to take control. Create the life he wanted.

He hadn't counted on the cute but weird local who had been behind him at the bakery. She'd certainly not been tuned into the idea of a relaxed pace. Donuts weren't his usual fare for breakfast so hopefully the chance of running into her again were slim to none.

Payton gathered his coffee and donuts and got out of the car. Unsure where to enter the building, he spied a sign stating it was the employees' entrance and started toward it just as a compact car whipped into the lot. He pushed the door open and found himself at the end of a passage that ran the length of the house.

Closing the door behind him, he headed towards the voices coming from the front. The floor creaked in places as he walked down the wooden plank hall. No serviceable white-tile floors of a hospital E.R. in sight. Along the way he passed small rooms located on the left side. Those had to be the exam rooms. Directly across from the third one was a small room that looked like an office. Next to it and just before the waiting room was an alcove that appeared to be the lab area. *Can you say go back in time thirty years?*

The end of the hall opened into a waiting room with a waist-high counter to the right that served as the reception desk. Chairs that looked like hand-me-downs from the hospital business office were pushed up against the other walls.

All talking stopped as he came into view. Three pairs of eyes fixed on him as he said, "Hello. I'm Dr. Jenkins, I hope you're expecting me."

Suddenly each woman started speaking. Finally, the middle-aged one with the red spiky hair waved a hand and the other two stopped. "Hi, I'm Jean, the office manager. This is Robin." She indicated the young woman to her left, who appeared to be fresh out of college and was smiling at him as if he were a candy bar. "She's one of the nurses. And this…" she pointed to the middle-aged woman sitting at the desk "…is Doris. She handles Reception. We heard you were coming and we're glad to have you."

"Thanks. I'm glad to be here. So we handle everything with one nurse?"

"Well, no. I don't know where China is but she should be here in a minute. It isn't like her to be late."

"Hey, someone give me a hand," a voice that was vaguely familiar called from the door through which he'd just entered. "You wouldn't believe the idiot in front of me at Dolly's," the disembodied voice said, dripping aggravation.

Down the hall came the woman who had been at the donut shop. Her attention was focused on maneuvering her way in the narrow space and she seemed to be struggling to keep several bakery bags and the purse that was slipping off her shoulder in place. Her chin-length, straight brown hair swung as she walked. She had a petite frame that made her almost seem fairy-like, especially dressed in hot pink scrubs.

The voice grew closer. "He took up two parking spaces. Asked Roger questions. Everyone in town knows not to ask Roger—" She came to an abrupt halt and her cocoa-colored eyes grew wide. "You!"

"Yes, I would be the idiot," Payton said in a voice that held a hint of humor.

There were soft chuckles from the other women.

"Wh…What are you doing here?"

"I'm Dr. Jenkins. The new doctor."

Eyes the same shade as the deepest part of the ocean twinkled at China.

Jean stepped forward. "I see you two have already met. Let me help with those."

China handed her the sack of donuts and the paper tray with four coffees. "I said I'd bring donuts," she murmured, unable to take her eyes off the doctor. How had she missed that shiny car in the parking lot? Because he'd made her late and she hadn't been paying attention.

"I can see," he said crisply. He looked at the coffee Jean held. "It looks like it was a good thing I stopped and got my own. You hadn't counted on me."

China's face heated. No, she hadn't. Why did he have to sound so gracious about it? To make her feel more guilty? The door behind him buzzed, preventing her from apologizing. She had never been so happy to see a patient.

"Dr. Jenkins, let me show you the office," Jean said.

"Robin will put the patient in exam one. When you're ready we can get started for the day."

The doctor gave China an unwavering look for a second before he followed Jean down the hall.

With relief, China sank into a chair next to Doris.

"Auspicious way to start the day," Doris quipped.

"Only you could use a big word to sum up total and complete embarrassment."

"Aw, honey. Such is life. Go do your job and all will be well."

The buzzer announced another patient. China opened the bottom cabinet and stored her purse. "I guess I'd better get busy before I look worse. Donuts and coffee will have to wait."

After Doris had taken the information from the mom of an eight-year-old boy, China led them to examine room two. There she took the child's vitals and noted the mom's recitation of his symptoms.

"The doctor will be in to see you in a few minutes," she said, before stepping out into the hall and placing the chart in a tray beside the door. As she turned to go to the front, she ran smack into a wall of male chest. A large hand cupped her shoulder to steady her.

"Are you going to be running into me all day?" a voice asked from above her head.

China stepped away and looked up at the insufferable doctor. "No. I'm sorry. I didn't mean to." China pulled the chart from the tray and handed it to him. "Your patient is waiting."

His low chuckle followed her down the hall. She shook her head. Obviously making good first impressions wasn't her thing.

China waited as Dr. Jenkins examined the boy and told the mom, "I'm going to have the nurse do a strep test and

see what we've got. I'll be back in after we know for sure."
He smiled reassuringly.

She followed him out of the room.

"It's China, isn't it?" he asked.

She nodded.

"Exam two needs a strep test. Where do I find those?"

"I'll take care of it."

China moved by him, taking special care not to make
contact. She went into the lab and he followed. "They're
right here." She opened the cabinet. "I'm, uh, sorry about
calling you an idiot."

He shrugged his shoulder. "It's okay. Sometimes I am."

Now he was being charming. She hadn't expected that.

"Thanks. I'll get this done." China held up the pre-
prepared swab with its plastic cap. "I'll let you know the
results right away."

Doris came down the hall. "China, your mom's on the
phone."

She wished she could make it clear to her mom not to call
her during work hours. "Please tell her I will call her back."

"I'll take care of the test if you need to get that," Dr.
Jenkins offered.

"No, I'll do it."

China waited for the doctor to come out of the exam
room where Robin had placed another patient. When he
stepped out she said quietly, "The boy has strep."

"Thanks for letting me know."

The rest of the morning passed in much the same way. At
lunchtime China and Doris took their meals brought from
home outside to the table. Robin and Jean would eat later.

"So how is Dr. Jenkins working out?" Doris asked.

"He seems to have a solid medical background, is great
with the patients and thorough."

"Well, that was certainly a clinical evaluation," Doris
remarked.

"I guess it was but I've not seen him do anything past strep and stomachache."

"Jean said Administration at the hospital told her he's from Chicago."

"Why would he want to come down here and work?" China picked up her drink and took a sip.

When Robin joined them China gathered her leftover microwavable lunch. She had to be on duty while Robin ate.

Jean called from the door, "China, Dr. Jenkins needs you in exam two. We have a boy with an open wound."

"On my way," she responded. "This may be where I get to see what he can do," China remarked to Doris as she hurried away.

China entered the exam room to find Dr. Jenkins with a lanky boy of about eleven years old sitting on the table and a mom perched on a chair with a troubled expression on her face.

"China, I'm going to need saline, a pan and a suture kit," he said, without looking up from his patient.

"Yes, sir. Right away."

He glanced up and gave her a quizzical look. A sharp tightness shot through her chest honed from childhood. What had she said wrong?

China left to gather the supplies. Returning, she found that Dr. Jenkins had turned the boy around so that he could place the pan on the pull-out footrest. There he would be able to pour the saline over the wound so it would run into the pan. China set the supplies on a small metal surgical stand that was stored in one corner then pulled it out to within easy reach of the doctor.

She opened the bottle of saline and handed it to him. He began to pour the liquid over the wound. When the boy winced Dr. Jenkins said, "I'm not from around here so tell me about this skimboarding you were doing."

The kid relaxed noticeably.

"It's done with a thin oval board. You throw it down and jump on it and ride it along the surf coming in on the beach."

"That sounds like fun. Are you any good?"

By this time Dr. Jenkins was preparing the local anesthesia to deaden the wound and the boy was taking no notice. The doctor had skills.

"Pretty good."

China had never learned to do anything like skimboarding, surfing or the usual water sports common for someone who lived near the water. Her father had become more controlling after her brother had left home at sixteen when given the ultimatum to straighten up or get out. China had learned early in life to do as she was told or she too might not have a place to live.

After her brother had left her father hadn't wanted China or her sister hanging out with the crowd down at the beach or doing much that wasn't under his watchful eye. Her mom, devastated by losing one child, had left most of the parenting to China's father. He'd had to know where they were at all times. "Might get into trouble. Too many drugs and alcohol. That's where your brother got into trouble," he'd say. China soon found that it was easier to just go along with what her father had wanted, to do whatever had kept the peace.

For Kelsey it had been much harder. As soon as she'd finished high school she'd been out of the house. Sadly, China didn't hear from her outside an occasional card or phone call. She missed Kelsey and wished they had a better relationship. Kelsey's hadn't spoken to their parents in years, which meant that her parents, especially her mom, clung to China.

"Do any tricks?" Dr. Jenkins asked, drawing China's attention back to what was happening in the room.

"I can turn around," the boy told Dr. Jenkins proudly.

"Wow. Do you think I'm too old to learn?" The doctor placed the needle at the edge of the boy's laceration.

"Naw, heck anyone can do it," the boy said, squaring his shoulders in pride.

"You think you could teach me?" Dr. Jenkins made the first stitch and the boy didn't even flinch.

"Sure."

"What do I need to know or buy?"

"It's no big deal. All you need is a board. You can get those anywhere around here."

"Do I need a special size?"

Was he really going to try skimboarding? That was for kids.

With a grin the boy said, "As far as I know, they only come in one size."

"Any certain weight I need to get?"

The boy gave him a perplexed look. "Not that I know of."

Dr. Jenkins tied off the last of the nine neat stitches he had placed in the boy's leg.

China had to give him kudos for a quick, perfect suturing job and keeping the patient calm. He had a wonderful way with the boy. She'd seen none do better. Actually, he was the best she'd seen.

Dr. Jenkins pushed the stool back and stood. "Would you teach me?"

He sounded serious.

"Sure, why not?"

"Great. I'm going to let Nurse China bandage you up. I want you to come in one week from now to have the stitches out. Then we'll make a date for you to show me how to skimboard."

"Okay," the boy said, with a huge grin.

He spoke to the mom. "Just see that it remains dry and clean. No swimming or skimboarding until the stitches are removed."

China began opening the sterile bandage package.

From behind her Dr. Jenkins said, "Let's not use that one. It needs a four-by-four."

That tightness in her chest was back. Was this doctor going to be hard to please? "I'll get one right away." She left and returned with the required gauze.

Dr. Jenkins stuck out his hand. The boy hesitated a moment and then took it. The doctor smiled. "See you next week. I'm going to hunt for a board today. I'm already looking forward to the lesson."

Who was this guy? He sounded like he'd moved here for the recreation instead of a job. He had an excellent bedside manner but would she be able to work with him?

Leaving the clinic for the day, China still had grocery shopping to contend with before she could go home. She hated it, hated it. The word wasn't too strong. She made a point to be in and out as quick as possible. Some people didn't like to clean bathrooms but shopping for food was her issue.

She maneuvered the buggy with the knocking wheels at a brisk pace through the aisles, snatching what she needed from the shelves. She tended to buy the same things so she didn't worry about studying the prices or nutritional value. It had been a long day, starting with the trip to the donut shop, and she just wanted to go home, maybe do some gardening.

With everything on her list except the trail mix she favored, she pushed the buggy through the produce department. She reached out to pick up the plastic bag of nuts, chocolate candy and oats.

"So, not after donuts this time, I see."

She looked up to find Dr. Jenkins grinning at her. She wanted to groan. Was he going to be around every corner she turned?

He moved his nearly full cart along beside hers. "I guess food is our common denominator."

"I don't think it's so surprising that we meet here since we've only shopped at the two busiest places in town."

"Still testy over this morning? Are you prickly to everyone when shopping for food or is it just me?"

His grin fed her annoyance. "Hey, I'm not prickly." She pushed her cart forward. He followed. "I just don't enjoy grocery shopping."

"You know, if I was a psychiatrist I might find some hidden meaning in that statement."

She was afraid he just might. The job of shopping and cooking had fallen on her at far too young an age. She hadn't complained. If she'd wanted to eat then she'd needed to fix it. Now every time she entered the grocery store it brought back unhappy memories. That's why she made a point to do most of her buying once a month. She picked up the small items she might need at a convenience store at other times.

China winced when he peered over into her basket, "Not much of a cook, are you?"

She glanced at all the prepared food piled there. "No. In fact, I hate it."

"I love to cook. Our cook, Ruth, taught me all I know. At least now that I've moved here I'll have time to enjoy cooking a meal."

Our cook. They'd certainly come from two different worlds. She'd been the family cook. If you could call theirs a family.

More from intimidation than need, China picked up a few apples and put them in a small clear bag. She tied it off and placed them in her buggy. Payton had managed to make her feel at fault twice in the same day. Once over calling him an idiot and now over her eating habits.

"At least *they* look like a healthy choice." He nodded toward the fruit in her buggy.

Obviously she didn't meet the grade with his man. "So do your doctoring skills extend to reviewing everyone's grocery cart?" she asked flippantly.

He chuckled. "No, but I do believe in eating right and encouraging others to do so also."

"Well, it must be working. You are so slim and trim."

He blanched then said, "I'll let you finish your shopping. See you tomorrow."

China watched him walked away. They hadn't gotten off to the best of starts. Maybe she wasn't giving him the chance he deserved. She looked down at the items in her cart. He hadn't been wrong about her meal choices at all.

Payton opened the door to his house, which was built in the old Florida architectural style with wide verandas and seemingly never-ending white stairs up to the front door and another along the side to the kitchen. The property was located along West Beach Road well outside of town. He'd specifically asked the realtor for something private, well away from the summer crowds, with large windows. The woman had done her job well.

The master bedroom faced east, giving him a bright morning wake-up call. The house was well worth the amount of money he'd invested in it. Payton had hired a decorator long distance to furnish it. He'd wanted it livable when he arrived but it still lacked the personal touch.

He sighed. His parents didn't understand his need to leave Chicago. In fact, his father was so disappointed that he could hardly speak to him. He no longer met his parents' expectations. Having lymphoma had made him re-examine his life. His new goal was to find out what he wanted. His parents still held out hope he would change his mind and come home. He was just sorry that his actions had put a wedge between them. He'd changed, and they couldn't deal with it.

The house was huge and Payton had no one to share it with, but that suited him fine. Janice wouldn't have enjoyed it here anyway. Too hot, too many bugs and *too* far from social engagements. She'd complained he wasn't the man she'd fallen in love with. Did she think people who feared they might die didn't change? The second she'd found an opening she'd been gone.

Pushing the side door open, he placed the first load of bags on the counter then he headed out for more. Ten minutes later and proud he was no longer puffing after walking up stairs like he once had, Payton had all the food in the kitchen. He hadn't totally regained his strength but it was quickly returning. China had reminded him that he hadn't completely found the robust man he'd once been yet. Some swimming and sailing would solve that issue.

Today had been the first time he'd worked a full eight hours in months. He'd been the one in med school who everyone had envied for his ability to work on little sleep. Not anymore, though, and especially not tonight. Good dinner, short swim then off to bed was his plan.

After putting the groceries away, Payton pulled out a skillet. He'd prepared a simple stir-fry, planning to eat outside to enjoy the weather. Unlocking the door to one of the many porches, he picked up his plate and drink then stepped out. He sank into a wicker chair with a comfortable-looking pillow. With a sigh, he propped his feet up on the small table in front of him, which matched the chair.

The cell phone resting against his thigh in his hip pocket vibrated. It would be his mom. She'd already called a number of times during the day and he'd been too busy to answer. Because she was a mom she worried. The old saying that you were always your mom's baby, no matter how old you got, was no truer than when you were sick. His mom had more than jumped into caretaker mode when he'd required help. Now he needed her to let go, for his sake as well as hers. Still, he couldn't bring himself to tell her to back off. That was one of a number of reasons he'd wanted to leave Chicago.

Some time later, his meal finished, he pulled his phone from his pocket and pushed the speed-dial number assigned to his mom. His chest contracted at the sound of relief in her voice when he said, "Hi, Mom."

"Honey, it's so good to hear from you. How're you doing?"

Payton told her about his day, the house and the town. He left out his two meetings with China.

"Well, at least it sounds like a nice place."

Payton watched as the sun became a half circle on the horizon. "It is. I'll call you in a few days."

"Okay." The wispy tone in her voice said she was still holding out hope that Payton would return to Chicago. That wouldn't happen. All he wanted right now was to regain all his strength and make the most of life. He'd start by calling the marina and seeing if his sailboat had arrived. On his first day off he would be on it. It had been far too long.

Gathering his plate and glass, he took them inside. He'd call around to see where he might go parasailing. He hadn't done that since he was a kid. It would be fun to try again. He'd be looking for a skimboard tomorrow.

He hadn't missed the surprised then disapproving look on China's face when he'd been asking the boy about learning to skimboard. It would be the first of many new things he planned to experience.

The corner of his mouth lifted. China had made his first day at work in Golden Shores memorable.

The next morning Payton rose early to take a run on the beach. The distance wasn't what he could have done months ago but he was pleased with his effort. He felt invigorated and ready to face the day. His mom had admonished him not to overdo it but Payton was determined to get back to peak health as soon as possible and put having cancer behind him.

As he came down the hall of the clinic an hour and half later he heard the women talking but there was also a deep voice mixed among them. Payton placed his coffee and sack lunch in the office and walked to the front.

Jean and Doris were sitting behind the desk. Standing beside China in front of them was a tall, lanky man dressed in blue scrubs.

"Good morning, Dr. Jenkins," Jean said.

"Please, make it Payton." He looked at everyone.

"Payton it is," Jean said with a smile. "This is Luke." She indicated the guy beside China. "He's one of the nurses that rotates in when either China or Robin have a day off."

Luke extended his hand and Payton took it. "Nice to meet you."

"You too," Luke said. "We're glad to have you around here."

The front door opened and a patient entered, ending their conversation. Over the next few hours Payton saw a steady stream of people, the highlights of which were a stomachache, severe sunburn and a twisted ankle. He loved it. This was nothing like the high-pressure, impersonal work he was used to. This was the kind of medical-care work he wanted to do. At least when a patient returned to see him he would recognize a face, maybe remember a name. Everything his parents couldn't understand. He no longer wanted to be one of *the* doctors in Chicago.

It was late afternoon when China handed him a chart. "The patient is complaining of vomiting, running a low-grade fever and weight gain."

Payton's chest constricted. It sounded so much like his

symptoms. The ones he'd put off addressing, along with the swelling in his neck, until it had been almost too late. Deep in his gut he'd known it was cancer, but fear hadn't let him admit it. That was behind him now. He had a new lease on life, and he planned to make the most of it.

"Dr. Jenkins? Are you okay?" Concern underscored her words.

China's hand resting on his arm brought him back to reality. "I thought we agreed it was Payton."

She looked at him far too closely. Could she read his apprehension?

He moved his arm and her fingers fell away. He'd had his fill of concern months ago. "I'm fine," he said, far too sharply. "What room is the patient in?"

China stepped back and her eyes flickered with a look of what struck him strangely as fear before she said in a businesslike tone, "Exam three."

Why would she be scared of him? He'd spoken more harshly than he should have but not enough to bring that type of look to her eyes.

Thankfully the patient had nothing more serious than an infection. Was he always going to overreact when someone came in with the same symptoms he'd had? For a second there he'd slipped and the all-too-perceptive nurse China had noticed. That couldn't happen again.

CHAPTER TWO

TWO DAYS LATER, China came in on the one to seven shift. Evening shifts were her favorite. Busy, with often interesting patients but it allowed her to get some gardening done in the morning. Her plants were where she put all her energy outside of nursing. It had been her way of escaping the unhappiness in her house when she'd been growing up and it had become her way of coping. She was a member of a couple of garden clubs in town and made the most of what she learned.

"Hi, there," she said to Robin and Doris as she approached the front desk.

"Hey," they chorused absently.

"So what's been going on today?" China asked, as she put her purse away.

Jean leaned toward her. "Nothing special. Robin's been mooning over Payton. She thinks all doctors are good looking, especially if they drive a nice car."

China sputtered in an effort to contain her humor. Evaluating a man's looks wasn't China's usual thing and particularly if it was based on a car, but she had to admit Payton was attractive beyond the average male. Something about him intrigued her. She'd dated but had never let a guy get really close. When a guy started making demands she backed off. She'd had enough of that in her life. Could a man ever understand her need to be a partner, feel secure? It certainly wouldn't be someone like the sports-car-driving, silver-tongued, charismatic Dr. Jenkins. Her mother had warned her about becoming involved with men like her father. More than once her mother had said she wished for her daughters an easier life than the one they would have with a man like their father.

Robin's shoulders squared and she gave Jean her indignant look. "That might be so, but it doesn't change the obvious. He's got the hottest car in town."

The sound of a throat clearing came from behind them. "I'm not sure that's a compliment as it sounds like I have a four-wheel personality," Payton said from the doorway of his office, before he stepped into it.

Robin and Doris giggled.

"We really do need to quit talking about him. He seems to always catch us," Doris hissed.

China had learned her lesson way before now.

Payton strolled up to the desk. "Robin, how would you like to go for a ride some time since you seem to like my car better than me? I'll even let you drive."

The young woman's face lit up. "Really? You mean that?"

"Sure."

"If anyone else wants to come along…" he looked at Doris and then China "…you're welcome too."

Robin said with a huge grin, "You have a date. I'm off now but will be back at seven when you close up here."

China and Doris laughed as Robin almost skipped down the hallway with pleasure.

"I wish I could make all the women I know happy that easily," Payton said, as he picked up a chart.

Was he talking about a girlfriend? It didn't matter. It wasn't her business.

At present there was only one patient at the clinic, a preteen with a possible broken arm. As China walked down the hall to check on the boy, the low rumble of male voices caught her attention. Larry Kiser, the doctor Payton was relieving for the day, was in the office with him. Why was she able to distinguish Payton's voice so clearly from Larry's, which she knew much better?

She entered the exam room and spoke to the mom, reassuring her. As she exited Payton stepped out of the office.

"I understand that the patient needs to go to the E.R. for a cast," he said.

"Yes. I'll take care of the paperwork right away and let the E.R. know they're on their way."

"Thank you, China."

"You're welcome, sir."

"You don't have to speak to me like I'm a drill sergeant. Yes, is fine."

"I was taught to say 'Yes, sir' and 'No, sir.' My parents told me it was a sign of respect."

He nodded. "I appreciate that. But it makes me sound old and rigid."

"I'm sorry. It's sort of ingrained in me. I'll make an effort not to, but I can't promise it won't slip out."

"Where I come from, 'Yes' suffices."

Maybe the reason he rubbed her up the wrong way was because they were from such different parts of the country. "I'll try," she said, heading down the hall and mumbling, "sir."

"I heard that."

She grinned. There was something about Payton that brought out the devil in her, as her father would have said. She so rarely let that happen but it felt good when she did.

Robin and Doris left for the day, with Robin once again promising she'd be back at closing time. Payton pulled his keys out of his pocket and jingled them. "They're here, waiting for you."

The patient flow increased then eased around dinner-time, which gave China a chance to catch up on some charting and clean out a supply cabinet that sorely needed it. At five Jean had to run out for a few minutes on an errand. As China worked she could hear the soft rumble of Payton's voice as he dictated in the office.

She was standing on a small metal stool on tiptoe, stretching to reach a box of alcohol wipes that had been pushed to the back of the shelf, when Payton said, "China, do you—?"

China jerked back, her foot slipping off the stool, and she fell backwards. Strong arms caught her around the waist and set her safely on her feet.

Shaking, she quickly moved out of his hold. "You scared me."

"I didn't mean to. You aren't hurt, are you?"

"No, I'm fine," she muttered.

"Good."

He sounded indifferent and she was still recovering from his touch. "Is there something you need?"

"Wanted to know if there's more printer paper some-where."

"Yes. Jean keeps it stored in her office. I'll get it."

"Just tell me where it is and I can find it."

"I don't mind." China headed into Jean's office.

"Do you always have to be the one who helps?" His voice had a tone of exasperation. "I've noticed you're the first to say you'll do it."

She turned and placed her hands on her hips. He really was far too critical. "You gained all that knowledge from just knowing me a few days?"

"Yes. It's okay to let people manage for themselves."

"I do. But it is also nice to help when people need it. And while we're at it, do you feel the need to tell everyone how to live or am I just special?"

He raised a brow, which gave him a perplexed look. "What're you talking about?"

"I'm talking about you complaining about my eating habits, my speech and now my behavior. Is that something that people from the North feel compelled to do?"

"I'm a Midwesterner."

"Whatever you are, we're here in the *Deep South* and we consider it poor manners to criticize others, at least to their faces." She'd lived on an unraveling rope most of her life where disapproval was concerned and she didn't want to come to work every day thinking it would be there also. She turned and stalked into Jean's office. With a clap of the cabinet door closing, she returned and thrust a ream of paper into his chest.

Payton gave her a bemused look that upped her anger a notch.

"Don't worry, I won't be doing another thing for you outside what's required as a nurse." Having no place to go, she hurried down the hall and out the back door into the humid evening air.

What was wrong with her? The man made her mad enough to punch something. Of all the nerve!

Payton wasn't sure what had just happened but he'd give China this—she had passion. He'd seen her aggravated at him at the donut shop, had recognized her being impressed with his skills with a patient, had seen her apologetic over her grocery cart contents but he'd never have guessed at the depth of passion that was bottled inside her.

He had just been teasing her when the conversation had started but she'd taken it and run. He'd hit a nerve somewhere and she'd exploded. That would be an understatement. He didn't think TNT came in smaller or more combustible packages. Did that translate into any other areas of her life? The bedroom perhaps?

Payton huffed. He'd gone far too long without a woman to be thinking like that. Janice had left him and then he'd been so sick. China didn't even like him. She'd more than made that clear.

He'd returned to his office when the door from the outside opened and closed. Seconds later the water ran in the small kitchen sink. After a while China passed his door, carrying a water can, and was headed for the front of the building. He'd noticed her the other day caring for the large, lush ferns on the front porch and the tropical plant in the waiting room. She even took care of the plants.

Being cared for was something he wanted nothing of. He was determined not to make dependency a crutch in his life, become a burden. That was part of the reason he'd moved to Golden Shores.

He and China finished the rest of the evening in the professional politeness of "Yes, sir" and "No, sir" on China's part. Instead of the "sir" being an address of respect, it grated on Payton's nerves. It didn't have the ring of sincerity to it that it had once had.

He ushered his last patient out and found China talking and laughing with Jean and Robin.

"I'm ready when you are, Payton," Robin cooed.

Payton almost groaned. He may have done the wrong thing by asking Robin out on a ride. He'd have to make it clear this was a friendly trip. China excused herself, saying she had to clean the exam room before she left.

Fifteen minutes later China was coming out of the back door as he and Robin drove away. She called China's name and waved from his open convertible. He didn't miss China's weak smile and half-lifted hand in response.

For the next week they circled each other in polite indifference. It did help that they each had a different day off. On the day they both returned and were assigned the morning schedule together, China gave him a civil smile and went about her job with her usual competence.

Just about closing time Luke popped his head into Payton's office. "Hey, Payton, we're all going out to celebrate Jean's birthday tonight. She wants to do karaoke at Ricky's. Want to join us?"

If he had been in Chicago he wouldn't have been caught dead in a karaoke bar. His mom and father, his sister even, would've been worried that his picture might show up in the society column of the paper. Somehow at this point in his life karaoke sounded like the perfect form of entertainment. Plus he needed something more to do with his time. The people he worked with seemed like a good place to start cultivating friendships.

"Thanks. That sounds...interesting."

"Seven o'clock at Ricky's. You know where it is?"

"It that the place on Highway 13?"

"Yeah, that's it. See you there."

Payton and China had finished with their last patient and he was headed out the back door when he saw China stocking an exam room. "Aren't you coming to Ricky's?"

"What?" she said absently, as she continued to put bandages in a drawer.

"Aren't you going to Jean's party?"

"Nope."

What had happened to the "sir"? He'd been demoted. "You're going to miss Jean's birthday party?"

"I have a garden-club meeting."

"I don't believe you. Isn't there an age limit for those clubs? You look to be well under sixty-five."

"I'll have you know I'm a member of more than one garden club."

At least she was speaking to him. He hated to admit it

but he'd missed their *discussions*. "You do surprise me. I guess Jean will get over you not being there."

A couple of hours later Payton pulled into the gravel parking lot of Ricky's. It was already filling up with vehicles. The red-brick building didn't look like much but he had the correct place. A large neon sign stood on the roof, flashing the name.

He pushed a button and raised the automatic roof on the car, got out and locked it. Maybe it hadn't been a good idea to buy such a conspicuous automobile. The car stood out among the pickup trucks and midsize sedans. A sports car fit his new found need to live on the edge, though.

Payton pushed through the glass door of the entrance and stepped into the dimly lit and noisy room. Not immediately seeing Luke or any of the women, he made his way to the bar. After ordering his first beer in months, he turned his back to the bar and watched the crowd. Just as he was getting ready to search further the door opened and China walked in with Luke at her side.

So she'd decided to come after all. His middle clenched. Were Luke and China dating? Why that would concern him he couldn't imagine. China had more than made it plain on at least one occasion that she wasn't awed by him on any level and barely tolerated him at work. Why he was giving it a thought he couldn't fathom. He had no interest in her and certainly no interest in being rejected again. Even if he let himself become seriously involved with a woman… He didn't think he'd ever let that happen. Those that stuck with you through thick and thin didn't come along often.

Despite his conflicting thoughts, China held his attention. This was the first time he'd seen her in anything but scrubs. She wore a simple blue sundress that made her look more like a waif than a siren. But somehow it fit her. Her shoulders were bare and her hair brushed the tops of them. Luke said something close to her ear. The smile she gave him was a little lackluster. Luke directed her toward the bar.

Payton stepped over to meet them. China's eyes darted from him to the crowded tables to the bar and back. Hadn't she been here before? Luke acknowledged him with a smile and a nod. China gave him a thin-lipped smile and looked away.

A waving arm drew their attention to a table near the front of the stage. Payton made out Jean's red hair. Next to her sat Doris and Robin. Luke led the way, making a passage for China. Payton followed behind. He couldn't help but notice the gentle sway of the fabric over her high rounded behind. She had nice curves that the scrubs had kept hidden.

Payton tore his thoughts away from China and concentrated on making his way to the table. Doris, Jean and Robin had large smiles of welcome on their faces as they reached them. He shouted, "Hello," over the din of music and melee and took the last available chair, which put him between Robin and China. Robin scooted closer.

Jean leaned over the table and spoke to China. "Thanks for coming. I didn't think you would. I know how you feel about these places."

Payton looked at China. She had a smile on her face but it didn't reach her eyes. Why didn't she usually come with them?

"Yeah, I was real surprised when she called me for a ride," Luke announced proudly, looping his arm across the back of China's chair. His possessive action made Payton tense.

The waitress came by and took their orders. Payton noticed that China ordered a cola, not alcohol.

He leaned in her direction to be heard. A sweet scent that suited her tickled his nostrils. Something floral. "You've never been here before?"

She turned toward him, which brought her lips within kissing distance. Her eyes grew wide and she stared at him. "No."

"Hey, who's going first?" Luke asked. His hand touched China's shoulder and she sat forward.

"First?" Payton asked.

"Yeah, to sing." Jean grinned.

"I'll do it if you'll sing with me," Robin said, looking at Luke.

"Let's go do it," he agreed, grabbing Robin's hand.

Minutes later they were on stage, crooning to a 1960s song from the karaoke machine.

Payton couldn't resist smiling at the horrible theatrics. He glanced at China. She had relaxed and eagerly clapped when they were finished. He wasn't sure if it was to be supportive or from relief that they had finished.

Luke and Robin returned to the table to a round of applause. As the night progressed others took their turn on stage. Payton found he was glad he'd come. This was as foreign to him as a visit to the moon would be, and he loved it. There was a freedom to laughing and enjoying himself without worrying about others' expectations. Close to eleven, Payton decided it was time to call it an evening and told everyone at the table.

"Oh, no, you don't. You haven't sung yet," Jean said.

"Yeah, everyone has to sing," Luke added.

"Come on," Robin joined in.

"I don't think…" Payton looked around the table. They all gave him earnest looks not to back down.

"We've all taken our turns at embarrassing ourselves, so you have to also," Doris said, with all the authority of a judge.

"Last call for karaoke," a man on stage said into the microphone.

Jean looked at China then back at him. "I guess that means it will be a duet. China, you haven't sung yet either."

Payton turned to China. She went pale and shook her head.

"Hey, we have a duet here," Doris called, raising her hand and pointing to Payton and China.

They shook their heads in unison. The man with the microphone said, "It looks like they could use some encouragement so let's give them a hand."

China's chin went to her chest and her shoulders slumped. Payton didn't even have to wonder if she was embarrassed. The crowd went into wild clapping, hooting and slapping the table. Payton leaned over and said to China, "I don't think we have a choice."

He stood and offered his hand. At least this would be one more experience he'd never had.

China looked at Payton's outstretched hand. Her heart drummed against her chest wall and her palms became damp. The crowd was still loud with its cheerleading. She hadn't sung in public since she'd been in the middle-school church choir. This was not the place she wanted to start again, and Payton was certainly *not* the person she wanted to share the moment with.

She arched her neck to look at him. His smile was reassuring. "Come on, let's get this over with." He closed and opened his hand.

China placed hers in his and his large, strong fingers curled around hers. He gave a gentle tug. The crowd had died down some, but when she stood the noise level rose again. Payton led her to the stage, not releasing his grip. She gained confidence from the simple gesture. They'd hardly spoken other than about patient care, and now they had to do something as personal as singing together.

A spotlight circled until it came to rest on them. "I don't

want to do this." Payton had to bend to hear her. She could only imagine the intimate picture they must be portraying. Panic crept through her.

"Come on, you look like you're going to a funeral. It can't be that bad." He grinned at her.

Payton looked comfortable with the situation. He probably frequented nightclubs regularly and did this sort of thing often. She was completely out of her element. She didn't go to clubs and certainly didn't make a spectacle of herself, singing karaoke. He acted as if this could be fun. Humiliating yourself wasn't fun.

Everyone in town would know about this by morning. Her parents would be horrified she'd even stepped foot in this place. They would be upset when they found out. This had been one of Chad's hangouts. One of those places she'd been forbidden to go after he'd left.

Some of her friends had used fake IDs during high school to get in. In college she'd been invited on weekends but she'd always made an excuse about why she couldn't. The only reason that she'd come tonight had been because she'd let Payton dare her into it. Now the worst was happening. She'd disappoint her parents after working so hard not to add to their pain.

The first strain of an old love ballad began. Could it be any worse? "My Endless Love."

She groaned loudly enough that Payton glanced at her. He no longer had a sappy grin on his face. In fact, he looked a little green. With rising satisfaction, she grinned. This might turn out to be fun after all.

The words to the song began to scroll on the monitor. Payton's tenor voice sang smoothly. "'They tell me...'"

He'd surprised her again. The man could carry a tune. She picked up the next line and he took the other. Soon China forgot that she was in front of a group, singing with a man she wasn't sure she even liked. She had became so caught up in the sound of Payton's beautiful voice. They harmonized together on the chorus.

On the second stanza, Payton grinned at her when it was her turn to sing. She slipped on the first word but pulled herself together and gave it her best effort. The noise in the room gradually ceased as they finished with a long drawn-out note. The crowd went wild. China glanced at Payton. A smile of pleasure brightened his face. She'd not seen that look in his eyes before.

Payton wrapped an arm around her waist and pulled her against his hard body. She circled his waist with a hand. Briefly she noted she could feel his ribs.

"I think they liked us," he said near her ear. "We should bow."

She nodded, overwhelmed by being so close to him and how much she'd enjoyed singing with him. Who would have thought? He led her into a bow.

"Ladies and gentlemen, I do believe that was the best we have heard tonight," the emcee announced. "Are you two a couple?"

China shook her head vigorously and stepped out of Payton's hold.

"Well, you could've fooled us," the man said, as China headed off the stage.

She made her way back to the table, not looking left or right, to pick up her purse. She had every intention of walking straight out the door. China pulled up short when she realized Luke was no longer sitting there. He was her ride home. Where was he?

China searched the area, horror making her heart beat faster. She needed to get out of here.

"You were great." Doris, Jean and Robin spoke in unison.

"Thanks. Where's Luke?" She looked from one woman to the other.

"He was on call. He had to go in," Robin said. "We're going over to the Hut and see what's going on there for a little while—want to come?" Robin asked.

China had no interest in going to another nightclub. "No. I think I've had enough excitement."

"I can take you home," a voice she knew far too well said from behind her.

Did she have a choice? A taxi would take too long. Walk? Her house was too far and it was too late. "I would appreciate the ride."

"Okay, let's go."

Payton seemed as anxious to leave as she was. Picking up her purse and saying goodbye, she made her way to the door. Payton stayed close behind her.

China took a deep breath as she entered the night air. The wind gusted around her, a sure sign that it would rain before morning.

"I'm parked over here," Payton said.

He strode through the parking lot but not so fast that China couldn't easily keep up. At the end of the row they walked between two cars and were at his vehicle. With a soft beep the doors unlocked. Payton opened the passenger-side door for her.

"You know, you really don't have to hold the door for me."

"I'm just being a gentleman."

"Thank you, then." She slipped down into the low seat. "I may need more help getting out than in."

He chuckled softly. "I can do that too."

Payton closed the door and went around to get in behind the wheel. Starting the car, he pulled out of the parking space and asked, "Which way?"

"Back toward the clinic. I only live a mile or so away."

Payton's vehicle really was nice. She ran a hand over the smooth leather of the seat. China knew luxury cars. Rob had had one when he'd wheeled into town. He had been a big-time real-estate man from Los Angeles, looking for investment property. He'd come by the clinic and taken a liking to her.

Always a bit of an outsider, Rob made her feel wanted, had filled her head with promises of being the center of someone's world. Just as quickly as Rob had arrived, he'd disappeared, leaving China crushed. Lesson learned. She rubbed the seat again. Payton's car and hers were one more thing they didn't have in common. The feel of the leather reminded her not to pin her hopes on someone. The small-town life, white sands and blue waters and especially her wouldn't hold a man. She'd accepted what her life was and would be.

She and Payton rode in silence as if they were both glad to have a reprieve from the noise inside Ricky's. Leaning her head back, she closed her eyes.

"Hey, don't go to sleep on me. I'll have to take you to my house if you do."

Her eyes flipped open and she sat up straighter. "Make a right one block past the clinic."

"So I'm guessing you don't want to go home with me."

China wasn't going to comment on that statement. She wasn't up to their usual conversation. He made the turn she'd indicated. "Go three blocks and turn left and the house is the second on the right."

Payton smoothly maneuvered through the tree-lined streets and pulled into her drive.

China opened the car door. "Thanks for the ride."

"Hey, wait a minute. I'll help you—"

"I've got it. See you later."

She was out and gone before he could open his door. He watched in the illumination of the headlights as she bypassed the walk to the front entrance of the bungalow and continued toward the detached garage further down the drive. Her dress blew in the wind that was picking up. He caught a glimpse of trim thigh before she pushed the hem back into place. Reaching the stairs, she started to climb them.

So China lived in the apartment above the garage. Flowerpots lined the steps. She really loved plants and seemed to have a green thumb. Maybe he'd been a little harsh with his comment about garden clubs. The plant care he was familiar with was done by someone who showed up in a van and brought new plants to replace the brown ones. Neither his mom nor Janice would ever damage their manicures by messing in dirt.

China was nothing like the other women he knew. She was a dependable nurse, helpful beyond necessary, gardener, a darned good singer, and she had the prettiest brown eyes he'd ever seen. What more was there to discover about Little Miss I-can-hold-my-own-in-a-battle-of-wits?

Payton waited until the light flickered on inside the area above the garage before putting the car in reverse and backing slowly out of the drive.

China was the most interesting woman he'd met in a long time. Did he want to discover more?

CHAPTER THREE

NEAR LUNCHTIME, ON TUESDAY of the next week, Doris stuck her head inside Payton's office and said, "Hey, Jean needs to talk to everyone. It's a slow day, which doesn't happen often around here so we're going to eat and meet at the picnic table out back."

She headed down the hall without waiting for a response. That might have been the longest invitation he'd ever received to lunch and he came from a society family who made them a regular affair. Doris, he'd learned, was the mother hen of the group. Robin the precious child they all tolerated, Jean the leader who used a kitten-soft hand but everyone heeded, Luke the fun guy who popped in, and China... He smiled.

Monday morning she'd arrived at work with no comment on their duet on Friday night. He'd overheard the other women teasing her but she had not said a word to him that hadn't been professional in nature. He would have thought she'd softened toward him after their evening out, but not China.

Still, it was a nice day and he looked forward to taking his meal outside with the others. He was slowly feeling more a part of this close-knit group. There had been none of the same camaraderie at the large E.R. he'd left. The staff had come and gone with too much regularity. Golden

Shores was slowly turning into a place he could belong. To make life even better, he'd just received a much-awaited phone call that his boat had arrived. Sailing topped his agenda for his next day off.

Payton stepped out into the bright sunshine and breathed deeply. He felt better just by being in it. He couldn't remember a time when he'd ever done anything like have lunch with co-workers, other than grabbing something from the machine on the way through the snack room. He wanted to live differently and this certainly qualified. There would have been no "Let's go out back to eat" if he was still in Chicago.

"Hey, Payton, we saved you a spot." Jean shifted around on the cement bench, giving him a place to sit. Doris sat next to her and moving around the table was Luke and beside him China. As he maneuvered his leg under the table his knee hit China's leg. Her gaze jerked to his before she lowered her gaze and pulled her leg out of contact with his.

He glanced at her lunch. She had a sandwich and raw vegetables. At least she didn't have one of those nasty pre-packaged microwave meals with all the preservatives. When she noticed his interest, she moved her meal more squarely in front of her but didn't meet his look. He couldn't help but grin. She was self-conscious.

"We've been asked to cover the medical tent at the concert Saturday night. I'm sorry that I couldn't give you more notice. I only do what the higher-ups ask. For your trouble you will all be awarded the next day off."

Everyone but him groaned.

"It's Sunday. That's our day off anyway," Luke said.

"I was hoping you wouldn't notice that." Jean smiled. "Our shift will be from eight until."

"Until?" Payton asked.

"Until it's over," everyone, including China, said in unison.

"Where's the venue?" Payton asked.

"On the beach near the state park. They put up a large stage and in comes the crowd," Luke offered between bites of sandwich.

"How do they charge and control the crowd?"

"Don't. This one is to encourage tourism around the Gulf area to help the economy after the tornado that came through last spring," Luke said.

Payton remembered it. He'd seen a little of the TV reporting when he'd been in the hospital, recovering from pneumonia.

"People are bused in from parking lots out of town. It's a big deal. And a lot of fun."

Jean held up a hand. "Now that Luke has given us an enthusiastic overview of the event we need to get down to the medical particulars. We should expect the usual. Too much to drink, falls, turned ankles, the occasional black eyes from hands being slung during dancing. I've already spoken to Larry. He and Robin will take the early shift."

She looked at Payton then China. "You two will have the late shift. You'll need to be at the tent no later than nine o'clock and stay to see that the tent is dismantled. That means bringing everything back here afterwards. Remember I said you get the next day off." She gave them a bright smile. "Doris and I will be splitting up to help with the paperwork. Let's plan for the worst and hope for the best."

China had always enjoyed working the concerts. She loved music and it was a great way to enjoy some of the best. The artists were world class and they were giving of themselves to help others.

An hour before she'd been assigned to arrive she stepped off the hospital shuttle bus. She'd left her car parked behind the clinic. China headed for the area where the medical tent was located. The warm-up act was already on the stage and the noise level was rising. Crossing the section of the beach highway that had been closed, she made her way to the entrance gate and showed her badge. As she walked, she passed food venders, T-shirts sellers and trinket hawkers. The excitement and intensity in the atmosphere grew the closer she moved to the stage. The medical tent had been stationed on a concrete area with easy access to the road in case an ambulance was needed and just far enough away from the major activity that it was easy enough to talk without shouting too much.

Larry and Robin were seeing to a patient as she entered. To her surprise, Payton was already there. He wore a polo shirt that hung loosely from his broad shoulders across his chest and a pair of tailored khaki shorts that made her think of preppy men and tennis matches. This was no -shirt with a slogan and slouchy pants kind of guy, the kind she tended to notice. If she had to pick a word for Payton's looks it would be classy and they had an appeal.

Her familiarity with guys like him was little to none. No wonder Payton seemed to rub her the wrong way so easily. She had no concept of his kind of guy, didn't know how to react to him. As long as he kept his criticism to himself, she found he had some positive qualities.

Payton was patiently putting a small bandage on the moving target of a two-year-old girl's finger. The mom was blissfully watching Payton, not her child. He seemed oblivious to the woman's admiration.

China had to admit it made an almost Norman Rockwell

moment. Payton's dark head, leaning over the little girl's blonde curls, had her wondering if he'd ever thought about being a father. He was good with kids.

Had he ever gone skimboarding? The boy had returned to have his stitches removed but she'd been with another patient and didn't know if they had really made plans. Not wanting to step over the line into personal space, she'd not asked. It was unlike her to be standoffish but every time she and Payton moved beyond the professional—Jean's birthday was the biggest example—things got too personal. Too uncomfortable. Payton seemed to be from the same mold as her father. She wanted no part of that.

Anyway, he was just another co-worker, and tonight he was more so as they would be partners.

Larry and Robin were still seeing to a patient when Payton finished.

"You're certainly here early," China remarked.

"Yeah. I wanted to see what was going on. I've never been to a concert on the beach. There really is a crowd."

"Yes, there is. I never did things like this either."

"Why? You live right here."

"I was too busy doing other things."

Cooking, cleaning, washing clothes. It had needed to be done and she had been the one to do it. Her mom had been locked in her grief over not knowing where her brother was to the point she hadn't been able to function.

Payton glanced around the tent. "I haven't had a chance to look around. We're not busy now and Larry and Robin are here for another thirty minutes so how about you give me a tour?"

"You go on. They..." she nodded to the others "...may need help."

"Come on, China. Quit making excuses. I'm not going to bite."

She huffed. "I know that."

"So have mercy on the new guy and show me around."

Not wanting to cause a further scene, China nodded her agreement.

"Even though you're not on the clock yet, carry a radio in case we need you," Jean said, from where she sat at a small table with a laptop.

Payton took the radio she offered.

China headed out of the tent. Why did he always manage to goad her into doing something she wasn't sure she wanted to do?

She circled and weaved behind the back of the throng toward the ocean.

"Hey, wait up," Payton called. "A tour guide is supposed to stay with the person she's guiding."

"And the group is supposed to keep up." She headed down the middle of the beach.

"Where're we going?" he asked, catching up.

"This is the best way to see things otherwise we'll always be fighting the crowd."

They walked through the sand until they got about halfway to the stage and she stopped.

"This is part of the state park area." She swept her hand around. "I guess you've seen it when it is empty. That over there…" she pointed "…is the Beach Hut. The wildest place on the beach. They have mini-concerts and dancing all the time."

"Do you go often?"

Her head whirled and she glared at him. He was serious. "I do not."

"You've never been?"

She shook her head. That had been more Kelsey's scene. They were as different as daylight and darkness but Kelsey loved her dearly. Missed her daily. Wished they had the relationship that they had once had as girls.

His look was one of pure disbelief. "Not once? Didn't sneak in as a teen?"

"No." That had been Kelsey's specialty. Thank goodness she hadn't gotten caught. It would have killed her parents.

"Well, well." He pursed his lips and moved his chin up and down.

"Just what does that mean?"

"It means that I thought you might be a goody two-shoes and you have just confirmed it."

Compared to him, she probably was. He struck her as someone who went after a good time, and she was the one who found a peaceful evening at home exciting. Kelsey would like him. "Someone needed to be the good kid in my family."

She suddenly had all his attention. "Why is that?"

Heaven help her, she'd said too much. She didn't want to talk about the past now or even later with this man.

"Come on, I'll show you the stage area." China started moving again.

They walked further down the beach and far enough that the crowd swelled out. They began to have trouble moving around without running into someone. China stumbled when the smooth sand rolled under her foot. A hand grabbed her arm, steadying her. Payton's hand.

"Thanks," she mumbled. When they reached the barriers the security guard stopped them. They flashed their badges, and he smiled and walked away.

"This really is a major production. I had no idea how large it was," Payton said.

"And it's a really great thing these celebrities do for the coast. They not only bring money in, they get us noticed in the headlines. We need to start back."

He nodded.

When they'd come up off the beach and had reached the area where the concessions were located, China sat on the low curb and begin taking off her tennis shoes. Payton followed suit and they emptied sand out of their shoes. Done, and standing again, Payton said, "Hey, let's grab a bite to eat before we go to work. I bet we won't have a chance later."

"You mean this type of food?" She waved her hand around at the tents and food trucks lining the way. "These menus rely heavily on frying, which might not meet the specifications of your discerning palate."

"My, do I sense some sarcasm in that question? Just so you know I can eat good, unhealthy food with the best of them on occasion, come on, I'll buy." He headed down the lane.

"I don't think so."

"You know you want some. It's just your type of food," Payton called back over his shoulder.

"Please don't imply that you know me so well."

He stopped and looked at her. "Oh, I would never make that mistake. Okay, if I can't convince you to eat with me then at least suggest which truck might be the best."

She pointed toward the bright orange moving-van-sized truck with slide-up sides. A large shrimp was painted over most of the passenger-side door and overlapped onto the hood.

"Sid's is the best."

"Then Sid's is the place. What do you recommend?"

She looked at him as if he had three heads. "No self-respecting Gulf coaster would have anything but shrimp, hush puppies and fries. Ours is the best in the world."

Payton stood amazed at how animated China became about eating at Sid's. This was obviously serious business to her. For once she wasn't uptight around him. He liked this China a lot, wished he saw more of her.

"Are you sure you don't want me to get you a basket?" Payton asked.

"I'm sure."

"Okay, but it sounds like your loss."

He stepped to the window but before he could place his order a man almost too large for the space he was standing in said in a booming voice, "Hey, my China doll. Come to have some of Sid's famous shrimp?"

"Not tonight, Sid."

"But you are my best customer," the man complained. His smile was so large Payton felt such there wasn't a single tooth in his head that wasn't showing.

"I know, but my…" she hesitated a second as if searching for the right word "…friend would like to have your shrimp basket."

So now China considered him her friend. He'd certainly moved up in the world.

"Shrimp basket coming up." Sid turned around.

"So I'm your friend now, uh?" Payton asked in a teasing tone.

"Only as long as you like the same kind of food as I do." She grinned at him for the first time ever where it really reached her eyes. He couldn't help but stare.

A flash of yellow caught his attention out of the corner of his eye. Flames filled the space in front of where Sid stood. A curse word ripped the air as the blaze grew. Sid backed away, at the same time dropping the metal frying basket. He held his hand and doubled over in agony. A guy in the truck with him rushed to the fryer with a fire extinguisher. After a couple of blasts from the container the flames died out. Steely-colored smoke billowed out the serving window. The smell of sodium bicarbonate filled the air.

"Sid!" China's shout of alarm added to the chaos.

"China." Payton caught her before she rushed inside the truck. "Run to the med tent and get us two bottles of saline and bandages."

She didn't argue or question, was gone before he could say another word.

Payton hurried to the end of the truck and entered the doorway left open for ventilation. As the air cleared he could make out Sid, holding his hand wrapped in his apron. He moaned with pain.

"Sid, I'm Dr. Jenkins. Let me have a look at that."

The man's face, which had been rosy minutes before, had taken on a pale pallor. Payton's lips tightened into a tight line. Burns like this hurt like the devil.

"Push that stool this way," Payton barked to the young guy pinned in the truck because Payton and Sid filled the space between him and the door. The young man did as directed.

"Sid, you need to sit. I don't need you to pass out on me."

The man took the seat, moaning softly, his face contorted in pain.

Payton glanced at the helper, gaining his attention. "Get some cool water, not cold. A lot. We need to get Sid's hand in it."

The guy did as Payton said without question, thankfully. The helper handed Payton a cooking pot filled with water.

"Okay Sid, I need to see your hand. Be careful when you take it out of the cloth. We don't want you to lose that skin covering your wound."

Carefully Sid unwrapped his hand from the apron.

Payton examined the red injured skin. There was no blister present. A second-degree burn at least. "I don't think this is going to require a trip to the hospital, but you were close."

They had just finished submerging the hand in water when China returned.

She entered and unceremoniously placed the supplies bundled in her hands on the counter. "I also brought some dry clothes."

He glanced at her. "Good girl." A look of surprise and then satisfaction flickered across her face. "We need to get the hand clean and dry. We'll have to work fast because it will hurt like hell when it is out of the water."

Payton sat on his haunches in front of Sid. China brushed Payton's shoulder with her thigh as she maneuvered around him in the tight space.

"How are you doing?" China put her hand tenderly on Sid's forehead, pushing the tuft of almost nonexistent hair back.

"I've been better," he said through clenched teeth. "This is the worst burn I've had in a long time."

"We'll have you fixed up in no time, and you'll be frying shrimp for me again," China assured him.

Payton watched the interaction with interest. China cared about this man. But, then, China cared about everyone. She tried to make things better for each person she met. His mom had shown that same type of compassion until he'd announced that he wanted to do something different with his life. Then she'd not been pleased.

"Okay." Payton brought their attention back to him. He nodded toward the young man with the stricken look on his face. "Sid, we're going to let your help step out of the truck before I get started."

China brushed past him again as she exited so the helper could get by. When the man was gone, China returned, her thighs brushing his shoulder again. The space was unquestionably too tight.

"China, get a pan and fill it with soap and lukewarm water. We're going to have to get all the oil off. We'll do this once and do it well, so put plenty of soap in the water."

China went to the tiny sink and did as Payton asked. Bringing the pan back, she maneuvered around the other pan and placed the one she carried on the floor.

"Sid, I can't lie. This is going to hurt, bad. As soon as I'm done, back into the cool water it'll go," Payton said.

Sid nodded. Sweat covered his forehead.

"Okay, China, hold the soap pan up."

She put a knee on the floor and bent the other, picking the pan up she'd just prepared and holding it steady. Payton lifted Sid's hand out of the water and placed it in her pan. Sid hissed.

"Hang in there, Sid." Payton begin to scoop water over the angry wrinkled skin of Sid's hand until all the grease had been removed.

A long sound of discomfort came from Sid as the air hit the wound.

Payton placed the hand back in the cool water. China sat the pan down on the floor, splashing soapy water on one of his shoes. She stood and put a hand on Sid's beefy back, slowly moving it in a reassuring pattern over his shoulders.

"Sid, I'm sorry but we'll have to go at it again," Payton said. "I have to run saline over the area just to make sure it is clean. We can't have it get infected. When you're ready, let me know."

China picked up the soapy pan, went to the sink and emptied it. She returned with the pan and grabbed the two dry towels off the counter where she had left them. Going down on one knee, she placed the towels on her leg and held the pan in position to catch the saline.

Payton gave her a nod and a reassuring lift to his lips. She returned a thin-lipped smile. "This time we're going to dry it off and bandage it. Dry and clean is the ticket to no infection," Payton explained to Sid.

He nodded and lifted his hand out of the water. "It's easing some."

The look on his face was telling a different story. "I'll give you something for pain in a minute and then write you a prescription for something a little stronger to take if you need it." Again the man bowed his head.

Slowly Payton poured the saline over the hand, making sure it went between the fingers. He took a towel from her thigh. She was the most intuitive nurse he'd ever worked with, having everything prepared and within reach. He patted Sid's hand dry and examined for broken skin.

"Believe it or not, it looks good. The pain should ease and it should heal well."

The man had his mouth so tightly pursed that his lips were white.

China took the pan to the sink and left it there. She returned and placed a hand on Sid's shoulder again and squeezed. It was a soothing gesture, not over-the-top dramatic. Janice hadn't been capable of doing something as simple as that, just being there for him. China didn't even have to say anything to let Sid know she cared.

She handed Payton the roll of gauze and he begin wrapping Sid's hand, making sure he went between each finger. He finished by encasing the complete hand in gauze. With a grunt Payton stood and stretched. He'd been in a squatting position for too long.

"Can I still work? This is one of our biggest money events of the year."

"I don't think you need to be the fry cook but you could sit here and give orders." Payton offered him a smile. "But that hand must remain clean and dry."

"That's the best you can do, Doc?"

"Yeah, that's it. And I want you to stop by the clinic on Monday morning and let me have a look at your hand."

"You'd better do as the doctor orders," China said, giving the man a hug. She wasn't showing pity but practical concern.

China wasn't someone who ran from a storm but stood

against it. He appreciated that about her. In fact, he was finding a number of things he liked about China.

"I promise," Sid said softly, giving her a one-handed hug back.

China gathered the leftover supplies. When she had them together she leaned over and kissed Sid on the forehead. "I'll check on you tomorrow."

Sid gave her a weak grin. "You don't have to do that."

"I will anyway."

Payton stepped out of the trailer and China followed. China stopped when they were a few feet from the truck. She had an earnest look in her eye when she said, "Thanks, Payton. I'm glad you were there when it happened. That man is important to me."

He shrugged his shoulder. "You're welcome. So how do you know Sid?"

"He was my father's best friend when I was a kid." She walked on as if she'd said all she was going to say. There was more behind that statement, he just didn't know what.

China and Payton were late arriving for their shift but it was for good reason. Sid's burn issue could have been far worse if Payton hadn't been on the scene to care for it so quickly and carefully. He'd been proactive and sure of himself. In an emergency he was just the type of person needed in a leadership position, someone you could depend on.

Her heart had soared at Payton's praise. They had been partners, each appreciating the other's abilities. He'd moved up in her estimation.

When they arrived at the medical tent there were three patients being seen and another two waiting. It was much like that for the next three hours until the concert wound down and the crowd made their way home. Even then Security brought a middle-aged woman who had slipped and twisted her ankle when trying to load a bus. It took another half an hour to stabilize the joint by wrapping it. Security saw that the woman and her husband got to their car.

She and Payton still had to pack medical supplies and break down the portable examination tables and chairs and return them to the clinic before they could go home.

"You ready?" she asked Payton thirty minutes later.

When he didn't immediately reply she glanced at him. She was worn out but even in the dim light his shoulders slumped and he was moving more slowly. He was exhausted.

"You okay?"

"Sure." Payton lifted a large plastic box into the back of the van. Minutes later, with everything packed, he closed the doors of the van. "I'll drive," Payton said.

China climbed into the passenger's side before he offered to help her. The extra time they'd spent with their last patient had allowed the traffic to lessen and they made it back to the clinic in good time, but it was still well past midnight. They unloaded and she put away the medical supplies while Payton stored the folding chairs and exam tables in a small storeroom near the back door.

She was more than ready to go home. They'd had a busier night then she'd expected. They'd not even had a chance to grab something to eat or drink. Done, she walked to the back of the building to see if she could help Payton. It had been quiet for some time so she expected to find him waiting in the office. He wasn't there when she looked so she continued toward the back door.

Payton sat on the floor with his back against the doorjamb, as if he'd slid down the wall. She rushed to him, kneeling beside him. "What's wrong?" Instinctively she reached out to touch his forehead. He turned away, not allowing contact.

"Go away. I'll be all right," he growled.

"Did you fall?" China looked for any obvious bumps or bruises.

"No, I didn't fall. Go on home. I'll be right behind you." He still refused to meet her gaze.

"I'm not leaving you like this."

"I don't want your help," he hissed.

"You might not, but you're going to get it. I'm positive you need it."

"I don't need anyone fussing over me."

"I find you sitting on the floor, and you think I'm fussing over you?" she asked incredulously. "What kind of nurse would I be if I left you here?"

His eyes were diamond hard when he said, "Go away. I'll be fine in a minute."

"No. So what happened?"

"I'm just tired and hungry."

"It looks like more than that to me. I think I should get you to the E.R."

CHAPTER FOUR

PAYTON WISHED CHINA would just leave. He felt humiliated enough as it was. Why wasn't he surprised that the stubborn woman wouldn't do as he asked? "I am not going to the E.R. for a little dehydration." His voice held a touch of disgust. "I was dizzy, that's all."

"Dizzy?"

"Is that the new nursing practice? Repeating everything the doctor says?" What would it take to get her to leave? Could he make her mad enough that she'd just go?

She blinked. Climbing to her feet, she said, "I'll get you a sports drink out of the break room. Then I'm going to examine you."

"I'd appreciate it if you would leave me some pride," he mumbled as she left. He hated being weak. How had be managed to let this happen? Not being used to warmer weather and no food had taken its toll and here he was in a pool of mortification. He'd worked hard to put those days of illness behind him, had started over with a vengeance. Yeah, right. That was working well at this moment.

Less than a minute later China returned with the drink and a stethoscope circling her neck.

"I'll drink this and be able to drive home. It's late. You need to be in bed." He took a swallow of the liquid.

"I'm not leaving you until I know you can get home safely."

"Go home. Doctor's orders."

"Really? That's the best you've got?"

The woman had spunk. He took another swallow of the drink. The quicker his electrolytes stabilized the sooner he could gather his pride.

China placed her hand on his forehead. Her fingers were cool and dry. Somehow he felt more invigorated by her simple touch.

In complete nurse mode, she picked up his wrist and checked his pulse. How many times in the last year had that been checked? He'd been poked and prodded until he couldn't stand it anymore. He'd turned into a nasty patient but he'd been unable to stop himself. Fed up, angry with himself and life, he'd lashed out.

"It's a little fast but within range." She pulled the stethoscope from around her neck. "I'm going to need to listen to your heart." She started undoing the second button of his shirt.

"Why, China, I had no idea you cared. You've hidden it so well."

She fixed him with a look meant to quell him. Instead he enjoyed it. A sure sign he was starting to recover.

China removed another button then slipped the stethoscope under his shirt and listened. She was so close she could smell the salt from the ocean in her hair. One breast brushed his arm as she moved the stethoscope around on his chest. Oh, yes, he was undeniably feeling better.

The look of concentration on her face made him question if she'd heard something out of the ordinary. Done, she pulled the stethoscope away.

Her eyes widened slightly. She'd seen it. She was close enough that he heard her suck in a breath. Seconds later she released it and it warmed his neck. She'd seen the small blue tattoo on his chest. Now she knew what he'd never planned to tell.

"You've had radiation." She stated it in a matter-of-fact way. There was no pity, no sadness, just plain acceptance of fact.

"Yes."

"How long ago?"

"Months."

She leaned away from him but didn't stand. "Why didn't you drink more tonight? Say you needed to eat? You have to take better care of yourself. You should have said something. Asked for a minute to get something to drink."

He grabbed the door facing and pulled himself up. "You sound like my mom." China jumped up and reached an arm out to help him. He shook it off. "Are you about done with the lecture? We were swamped and you expected me to sit down and enjoy a meal. Give me more credit than that. I'm going home, China. You should too."

Payton placed a hand on the wall to steady himself and took another draw on the sports drink.

"You're not driving yourself home."

"How do you plan to stop me?"

"I'll call the police if I have to." She gave him a determined look that made him think she just might.

Too tired, too out of sorts and desperately wanting his bed, he nodded his agreement. "Okay. But you have to promise not to tell anyone about this or that I've been sick."

"Agreed. You wait here while I turn off the lights."

Payton did as he was told, no longer up to fighting with her. Soon she was back and they headed out the door. She offered to help him but he refused. It was bad enough she had to drive him home. He wasn't sure how he'd face her on Monday morning.

When China started toward her car he said, "No way am I going to fold into that tiny car. You drive mine."

She looked a little unsure for a minute then nodded. He dug out his keys and handed them to her.

As she pulled out of the parking lot she asked, "Where to?"

"West Beach Road. Five point three miles on the right. Three-story facing the ocean."

As he leaned his head back and closed his eyes he heard her low whistle. "Nice real estate."

Payton didn't know how long it took China to drive him home because he slept the entire way. It wasn't until he felt a gentle shake on his shoulder that he woke.

"I think you're home. Is this it?" China asked, looking out the front window.

"Yes." Payton reached for the handle and pushed the door open. "See you later."

"I'm coming up. With all those steps I want to make sure you don't fall."

Payton said a sharp word under his breath. "You're determined to emasculate me."

"I don't think that's possible. Your self-esteem and women's reactions to your good looks won't let that happen."

"So you think I'm handsome?"

"I'm not having this conversation at one a.m."

He stepped out of the car and started up the staircase. The thump of China's feet told him she was close behind. Guilt washed over him. She had to be every bit as tired as he was and she was babysitting him. He flipped the mat back and pulled the house key out from under it. Opening the door wide, he went in and flipped on a light. "Okay, now you have seen me home you can go. I'll get a ride in tomorrow and pick up my car."

"You plan to get a shower?"

"Why? You want to join me?"

She looked at him with a smirk. "No, but I don't want you to fall and have no one here with you."

"How do you know there is no one here?"

With satisfaction he watched her turn red. "I don't. I just assumed because you have never mentioned anyone…"

"China, there's no one here. You don't need to feel any obligation to stay. I'll be fine getting a shower. Go on home."

"I'll just wait."

After a huff of impatience he moved closer to her. "I want you to leave me alone."

"I will when I know you're safe."

He shifted so close that her breasts were only inches from his chest. She sucked in a breath and her eyes widened. "You can't intimidate me."

"I'd bet I can." Payton wrapped an arm around her waist and pulled her against him. His mouth caught the small sound of astonishment that escaped her lips before he covered them with his. Her lips were warm and full, wonderful. Her hand grabbed his shirt at his waist as if she needed to steady herself. After a few seconds she leaned toward him.

Payton let her go almost as quickly as he'd held her. He looked into her eyes. "I may be sick but I'm not dead. It has been a long time for me so don't come and check on me before you leave unless you plan to stay."

The next morning the sun was high enough in the sky it was becoming warm as China drove Payton's car toward his house. Had she gone crazy? Unable to stand not checking on him, she tamped down her nervousness. She'd made up her mind it was necessary and started driving.

He'd actually kissed her the night before. Why? Had she pushed him too far? Had he been trying to scare her so she would leave him alone? If that was the answer it had worked. He was walking down the hall when she tore out the back door. She'd run like the proverbial rabbit.

She had worried all night that something might happen

to him and now she'd made a fool out of herself by checking on him. In order to stall, she'd stopped to buy donuts. Before leaving home, she'd pulled some of her homemade chicken soup out of the freezer. If he wasn't into the questionable nutrition of donuts, maybe he'd appreciate the soup for lunch.

The sports car's tires crunched against the shell drive as she pulled in and stopped beside the stairs. Turning the vehicle off, she rested her forehead on the steering wheel in an effort to gather her wits. What was she going to say? *I was worried about you.* He wouldn't like that. He'd made that clear. Maybe *I just thought you might like breakfast. I brought you your car back. I loved your kiss, and I came out for more.* No, she *wouldn't* say that.

She raised her head, took a fortifying breath and opened the car door. As she placed a foot on the drive, a deep voice said in a sarcastic tone, "I was beginning to wonder if you were ever getting out."

China jumped. Her heart racing, her hand went to her chest before her gaze jerked upward, "Oh, you scared me."

"What're you doing here?"

He wasn't happy to see her. Okay, what was her plan? "I thought I may as well drive out and return your car. You can just take me home."

"Is that nurse-speak for 'I'm here to check on you'?"

"Yes. No. Maybe."

"You couldn't help yourself, could you? You have to make sure everyone is all right, taken care of."

China started up the stairs again. "Here I was trying to be nice and considerate. I brought your precious car back in one piece and brought you some donuts, plus chicken soup."

"Chicken soup? So you do think I'm an invalid. I don't need your pity, China."

She reached the porch where he stood glaring down at her. He was dressed in a pair of sport shorts and a T-shirt that had seen better days. Despite that, he looked heartier than he had the night before. She kind of liked the not so buttoned-up version of him, despite the snarl on his face.

"Please, don't mistake my concern as pity. I pity people I don't know. You're too aggravating to pity. So you can get over that idea."

His lips lifted slightly.

"I'll leave these for you." She indicated the donut box and bag with the soup in it. "I'll also call someone to come and get me. I'll just put these on the kitchen counter. You'll never know I was here."

His eyes moved slowly upward to meet her gaze and down her body again. "I doubt that."

Heat filled her. Was he referring to last night? China didn't know how to respond or if she wanted to, so she opened the door they'd used the night before and went inside. She placed the food on the counter. Was he trying to frighten her away? She refused to react to his poor behavior.

"Sorry to be such a grouch." He stepped over and picked up the donut box. "How about sharing these with me? Or I'll take you home, if you want."

Why didn't she jump at the chance? Maybe because she found this proud man interesting? He certainly kept her on her toes mentally. Since he'd come to town it had been one usual day after another.

"I guess I could have a donut since you asked so nicely."

"Good. Then why don't we eat these out on the porch? You want something to drink? Coffee's made."

"I'd just like a glass of water. I'll get it if you'll tell me where to find a glass."

"On the right side of the sink." He headed out the door. "I'm starving."

China found a tumbler, ran water into it and put in a couple of ice cubes. She considered the large kitchen area. She'd not paid much attention the night before, having been more concerned about Payton. The room was beautiful, decorated in a beach motif with a modern twist. It had bright blue round placemats on the oversized table that would accommodate a large family. Yellow and white striped curtains adorned the windows but didn't block the light. She liked it.

Picking up her glass, she went out to the porch. Payton sat on a settee with his legs stretched out over a table and the box of donuts on the cushion beside him. He had a blissful look on his face.

China took the chair to his right. He picked up the box and offered it to her. She pulled a donut out and gazed out toward the water. This area wasn't overly populated, like her part of town. She now knew why he had chosen to come out here and eat. The view of the ocean was amazing, wide and unobstructed.

Neither of them said anything. In some ways it was the most pleasant morning China had ever spent but in other ways it was the most disconcerting. The undercurrent of awareness between her and Payton made her feel edgy, insecure.

"I like your view," China finally said.

"Thanks. I've never really thought about it."

"How could you not?"

"I liked the house because it was far enough out to be private."

"Well, you sure got a view whether you value it or not. I've lived in Golden Shores my entire life and never had one this wonderful."

"Feel free to stop by and enjoy it any time."

She wouldn't be doing that. At least, not when he was home. "The house is plenty big enough for your family to visit."

"I don't see them coming down."

For a second a look of regret cross his face but he soon

recovered. The tone of his statement had her thinking that was a subject he didn't want to talk about any more than he did about having had cancer.

"You and your family are pretty tight, aren't you?" he asked.

"I am with my parents. I don't see my sister regularly." That was an understatement. "Do you see your parents often?"

He looked away and out toward the ocean. "I did when I was in Chicago but now that I'm down here obviously not much. I talk to Mom off and on, though."

"What about your dad?"

"He's not really speaking to me these days." He raised a hand, palm up, stopping further questions. "Which is something I'm not going to discuss."

So that was a touchy subject as well.

"Payton, why did you decide to move to Golden Shores? Outside of tourists, we aren't on anyone's radar."

"I wanted to make a change in my life."

"Because you've been sick?"

"You can call it what it is, China. Cancer. Lymphoma."

"Okay, because of the cancer." She still had a hard time saying the word.

"That and other things. The cancer made me see that I wanted to live life instead of spending my time climbing the career ladder at work or the social ladder outside work."

"Well, you've come to the right place for that. The only ladders I know of around here are the ones behind the sheds of people's houses."

Payton threw his head back and laughed. China joined him.

He slowly recovered. "That statement is just the reason why I am here." He looked at her long enough to make her squirm before he said, "You know, I think that's the only time I've ever heard you laugh. You should do it more often. You have a beautiful one."

Suddenly the conversation had turned personal and China wasn't as comfortable.

He continued, "I just want to work and put the cancer behind me. I moved down here to make a change for the better. I don't want people to feel sorry for me and I don't want to be treated differently."

"If you are talking about last night, we all need help some times. It isn't a bad thing to let others in."

"I had no intention of doing so. I would have never told you if you hadn't seen…"

Time to change the subject. "I put the chicken soup in the refrigerator. If you don't want it, just throw it out."

Payton looked at her. "I thought you didn't cook."

"I never said I didn't cook. I just don't like to cook." China took a bite of a donut.

"I see."

"It's my grandmom's recipe, if you must know. I make a batch up and freeze it. So it was no big deal to bring it."

"I appreciate you thinking about me."

Warmth filled her. He did sound grateful. There was a first time for everything. "You look like you're feeling much better. Did you have any trouble last night?"

He pierced her with a look that made her glow inside. Had he thought about their kiss? "Um, do you think you could take me home now? I'm supposed to be at my parents' for lunch."

"Sure, give me a minute to change. I'd planned to go sailing today anyway." He stood and gathered up the donut box.

"Do you think you should? After last night?"

A horrified looked marred his handsome features. "I'm fine, China. I just got a little dehydrated, that's all. Please, don't make more of it than there was."

"I just—"

"I know. You just can't help yourself." He moved around the table and passed her in one lithe movement that implied he was in perfect health.

China had to admit that over the past week he look like his skin had taken on a golden hue. As ridiculously aggravating as she found Payton at times, she liked him. He'd added excitement to her rather dull life.

"Let me get my shoes and gear. I'll drop you by your house on my way to the boat."

"You own a sailboat?"

His eyes lit up. "Yeah. A thirty-footer that is so sweet."

What would it be like to have Payton look at her with that same gaze of happiness? Why would she care? They just barely tolerated each other. The only time they seemed to work seamlessly was while caring for patients, and kissing. She shouldn't think about that.

"You need to be sure to drink plenty of water and wear your sunscreen. You don't want to relapse."

"China…" his gaze locked with hers "…stop it. I'm fine. I'm not one of your projects."

"I'm sorry. It just comes out sometimes."

"Forgiven this time. I'll get my stuff and be ready to go."

While Payton had disappear into his house, China took her tumbler inside and put it in the kitchen sink. Unable to control her curiosity about the rest of his home, she moved to the archway that separated the kitchen area from the living room. It was the most beautiful room she'd ever seen, with all the glass windows bringing in not only the sunlight but the view of the Gulf.

She ran a hand along the arm of one of the two blue overstuffed sofas accented in red. They faced each other in front of a framed large-screen TV above the fireplace. The high ceiling and slow-moving fans gave it an overwhelming feeling of comfort. Her breath caught as she moved further into the room. Before her was a grouping of comfortable-looking chairs covered in a sand-color fabric that faced the ocean. Stepping over to one, she marveled at the one-eighty-degree view.

The only thing missing to make the room perfect was greenery, something living. In her mind's eye she placed a Hawaiian ti near the chairs, crotons in a bright spot on the end table and a majesty palm in the corner. She smiled. Perfect.

"Hey, I was looking for you. Ready to go?"

Payton looked healthy in his white knit shirt and navy shorts. He wore docksiders on his feet. The quintessential yachtsman, if she'd ever seen a picture of one.

China glanced down at her pink T-shirt and blue jean cutoffs. They were definitely from two different worlds. She would go shopping this week and do better with her dressing.

"Just waiting on you."

"You had a funny look on your face when I came in. Is something wrong?"

"Just daydreaming."

He came to stand beside her. "I wouldn't have taken you for a daydreamer. I see you as far more practical than that."

"Maybe I'm full of surprises."

He wrinkled his brow in thought. "Maybe you are at that. Uh, about last night. I know I overstepped the boundaries with that kiss. I hope you don't think that's going to happen again. I'd like us to be friends. I don't what that to stand between us."

She swallowed. Obviously he hadn't reacted to that moment like she had. China mentally shook herself. Payton was a co-worker and the type of man she needed to be involved with on a personal level. They were professionals and it needed to remain that way.

"How about we start over and try for friends?" Payton offered.

That sounded safe enough. She smiled. "Friends sounds good to me."

Payton wasn't so sure he was completely comfortable with China's ready agreement to them just being friends. He shouldn't have kissed her but, still, he had enjoyed it. It was just as well they didn't become more involved. She knew too much about him. What if he started to care and she realized she couldn't deal with his health issues? No one would have that kind of power over him again. Remaining friends was a good plan.

He pulled into China's drive. "Who lives here?" Payton indicated the house.

"Mrs. Waits."

Payton studied the yard and the lush greenery around the house. "You do her gardening for her, don't you?"

Taking on a bashful look, China said, "I help her."

"You have a green thumb. The yard is beautiful. Would you consider helping me with my place? Pick out a few plants?"

A glow to compete with the lights of New York on a clear night came over her face then faded. "I don't think I can."

She didn't need to get mixed up with him. Despite appearances, he might leave just as quickly as he'd arrived. What kind of person just picked up and left everything they knew and loved? Her brother had but, then, he'd just been a kid. Kelsey had in every sense of the word, except the physical. Did the fact she was still in town give her a chance to get to know her sister again?

"Why not?" Payton demanded. "I can see you want to."

"You can't."

"China, can't you help out a guy that's clueless?" He

made a pitiful face. "We could go shopping on our next day off. Have a friendly outing."

"Outing? That sure is an old-fashioned word."

"It's a friendly word. Like one friend helping another pick out plants."

"You're not going to give up on this, are you?"

"I'd rather not."

She grinned. "Okay. I'm off Thursday. How about you?"

"Yep."

"I promised to help my mom that morning but I'm free that afternoon."

He tapped the steering wheel with his palm. "Then it's a date. I mean, a friendly outing."

China looked as if she might back out for a moment before she said, "I'll be ready." She opened the door and stepped out but leaned down again to look at him. "See, it isn't so hard to ask for help."

"Are we back to that?" He didn't want to talk about what had happened last night.

"I just don't want you to get into trouble."

He grinned. "So what you're saying is that you care about me."

"No. What I'm saying is that even I would stop and help a dog if it was hurt."

Payton couldn't contain the laugh that burst from him. "So is that a move up or down, in your estimation?"

She glared at him. "Bye, Payton."

Payton was disappointed to hear the car door click closed. The sudden silence wasn't as peaceful as it had been before China had come into his life. He drove away with a feeling flooding him he'd not experienced in a long time—happiness.

He'd made the right decision. Their kiss the night before hadn't been his smartest move. China was the type of woman he had no business trifling with. She was permanence, stability, and he'd just come out of a hurtful relationship with no intention of returning to one any time soon. China, of all the females he knew, wouldn't accept half measures. She was marriage, a house, car and two children sort of person. He wasn't that guy, at least not anymore.

At one time he'd believed that he and Janice would settle down together and have a family. His illness and her inability to deal with it had ended that dream. Now all he wanted was to make the most out of life, live to the fullest. To stay away from anything more emotional than how he felt about his boat. If he did get involved with China and they became serious, she'd be the type to stay with him out of guilt if he became sick again and he wouldn't accept that, on any level.

The next morning Payton arrived at the clinic feeling better than he had since he'd been told he had cancer. Yesterday's sail in the bay had been stimulating. It had felt good, being active again. Despite his aggravation with China, he'd done just as she'd instructed and made sure to drink plenty of fluids and wear sunscreen.

Leaving his lunch in the office, he made his way to the front to check in for the day and was disappointed to find that China wasn't standing at the counter, as was her habit.

"Good mornin', Payton."

"Morning, Doris. Any patients for me this morning?"

"Not yet, but I'm sure we'll have one soon."

"Hey, Payton," Robin called, as she came out of Jean's office.

"Good morning." He worked to keep his regret off his face. If Robin was working the early shift, China wouldn't be in until two.

Going through his usual routine for the day, Payton caught himself checking his watch more often than he was comfortable with to see if it was time for China to come in.

He'd managed to ask discreetly if it was her or Luke who would be there that afternoon.

His heart beat faster when China's voice carried down the hall from the front as he came out of an exam room. This wasn't good. The woman had become an infatuation he couldn't afford. He was making more of a few cordial moments on his porch the day before and his ability to convince her to help him buy plants. For heaven's sake, he'd never cared about a plant in his life. Had all that chemo affected his brain? He was enamored with China and he was acting like a schoolboy on Valentine's Day.

He had to put a stop to it. Someone who was easy and uninvolved was what he was interested in. That didn't describe China. He didn't want to hurt her, and he would if he continued on this path. So why had he been looking forward to seeing her with such anticipation? It was time to find some female company that wasn't China. Plan made, he was out of the clinic in thirty minutes.

Payton was on his way to the front desk when a booming voice said, "My China doll."

Sid. Payton couldn't help but grin. The man was a character.

"Come on back," China said. "I'll find Dr. Jenkins and let him know you're here."

Payton met them coming down the hall. He had to force himself to take his gaze off China. He was going out tonight to meet some women. "Hi, Sid. I thought I might have to go to the restaurant to check on your hand."

"China told me to wait until she was here. She said you'd still be around."

"Good. Come on in here and let me have a look." Payton headed into an examination room. Sid followed and China came in behind him. "So, have you been keeping it clean and dry?"

"The best I can," the older man said in a noncommittal tone.

Payton gave him a pointed look.

"I've not been cooking, I promise. I do have to take a bath sometimes, but even then my wife made me wear a plastic bag over it."

Payton smiled. "Understood." He turned to China. "Please get some antiseptic liquid. I'd like to rinse Sid's hand in that just to make double sure it doesn't get infected. Then I'll rebandage it."

China nodded and left.

Sid watched China leave. "That's a good girl there. She sure hasn't had it easy."

"I'm afraid I don't know her that well. Let me see you hand."

Sid swore and lifted his injured hand. "With China what you see is what you get. Pure goodness through and through."

"She is nice." Payton found that he meant that. Too much so. China had been great to him when he'd been sick and had cared enough to go out of her way to check on him yesterday. Against his better judgment, he liked her attention.

"Smart too. Top in her class at nursing school and while taking care of her family."

Panic filled him. *China has a husband? Children? No one had ever said anything. Had he kissed a married woman?*

"I didn't think China was married." The statement came out with a little waver in his voice.

"She's not, but her parents depend on her. Still do. Far too much, in my opinion. Since she was twelve until she moved out last year, she's pretty much held the family together."

Relief filled Payton as the last of the gauze dropped into

the garbage can. Seconds later China entered with a plastic bottle in her hand and bandages in the other.

"It looks like you hand is healing well. Continue doing what you're doing, Sid. China, I'm going to let you handle washing Sid's hand and the rebandaging," Payton said.

At China's surprised "Okay," he glanced at her. Hadn't she ever been trusted to do more?

"We good?" he asked her.

She straightened. "I'll take care of it."

Payton headed toward the door. "Good to see you again, Sid."

"Hey, I want to give you these." The man handed Payton some cards. "A couple of free meals on me in thanks." He nodded his head toward China. "Maybe you and China can come in together."

"Sid." China tried to shush him.

Had China told Sid about Payton kissing her? No, that wasn't something she'd share.

"Thanks Sid, I might just do that. Take care of yourself."

CHAPTER FIVE

A FEW MINUTES later Payton joined China in the hall as Sid headed for the front door.

"How does it sound if I pick you up at two on Thursday?"

China looked behind her. Had anyone heard? She didn't want the others to know that she and Payton were doing something together. They would make more of it than there was.

"You're not thinking of backing out on me, are you?"

She was but she didn't plan to tell him that. "Uh, no. Two sounds fine."

"Good, I'll see you then." He strolled toward the employee entrance.

China groaned when Robin came out of the back room. Telephone, telegraph, tell Robin. Now everyone would know she and Payton had plans.

"So, you and Payton have a date?"

China managed to turn a groan into a low moan. "No date. He just wants me to help him buy some plants for his house."

"Well, that's a new twist on 'let me show you my etchings'. I thought you didn't even like him."

"I never said that. Anyway, it doesn't hurt to be nice to a new person in town. Show some southern hospitality."

Robin gave her a knowing grin. "If you say so."

Against China's better judgment she was starting to like Payton, far too much. That kiss that gotten her to thinking what if... More than once Payton had proved that he wasn't the controlling person that her father was. Just now he'd handed over Sid's care, believing she could handle it without him looking over her shoulder. It was a simple thing that signified what he thought of her abilities and that meant the world. She'd grown up with a father who'd ruled with a thumb firmly on her, no trust. She smiled. Payton trusted her at least with his secret and patients.

China still had that smile hovering around her lips when Doris said, "I hear you and Doctor Hunky have a date?"

"Doctor Hunky? When did you start calling Payton that?"

"So you think he's hunky too?"

Doris was watching her far too closely for her reaction. "I didn't say that!"

"You didn't have to. You knew exactly who I was talking about." Doris grinned at her.

Jean came out of her office. "So what's this I hear about you and Payton dating?"

China put her hands on her hips. "It's not a date. He asked me to lend a hand in finding some plants for his house."

Jean nodded. "Well, he asked the right person."

China could have kissed the woman. She at least accepted the idea of her helping Payton without any strings attached.

"Have you ever been to his house?" Doris asked.

China hated to lie but she'd promised Payton she wouldn't tell anyone about the cancer. If she admitted she'd been to his house they'd want to know why. "No, but I guess we'll go there before we go to the nursery."

"I heard it's the big yellow one down on West Beach Road. I've always wondered what it looked like inside."

"Then maybe you should come for dinner some time," Payton said from behind them.

All their heads swivel to the sound of Payton's voice.

"I thought you'd left," China blurted. What had he heard of their conversation? Her lie?

"I forgot my lunch box. I just stopped back to pick it up."

Doris shook her head. "This is the last time I'm going to talk about you without letting you know first, or maybe I should put a cowbell around your neck so I'll know when you're coming."

Payton chuckled. China liked the sound.

"I'll try to stomp my way up the hall from now on. About that dinner. How about Saturday night at eight?"

Embarrassment covered Doris features. "I can't have you do that."

"Would you agree if I invited you all to dinner?"

Doris looked at her and said, "China, you'll come, won't you?"

She didn't know how to gracefully say no, and Doris was giving her a pleading look.

"I guess. I usually spend time with my parents on Saturday night, but I can change it to another night."

"Great," Payton said. "I'll see if Jean and Robin can make it. Maybe Luke and Larry."

The more the better as far as China was concerned. That way the larger the buffer between them. He'd given her one more reason to like him. Payton had to stop that. What was she going to do when she had to be alone with him on Thursday?

By the time Payton arrived to pick China up three days later she'd worked herself up into a nervous tizzy. She'd changed clothes five times. Even more times she'd picked her phone up to call to say she couldn't make it. Instead, she made up her mind that she was an adult and could do something as simple as going to a plant nursery with an attractive man.

She was sitting on the bottom step of the stairs to her apartment, waiting, when Payton pulled into the drive. Her traitorous heart fluttered as he grinned at her when he climbed out of the car.

He wore jeans that had seen better days, a blue collared shirt and his docksiders. His hair had grown to more of a military length. Pink colored his high cheekbones. He'd been in the sun earlier in the day. Payton looked the picture of health, and she'd never wanted to kiss a man more.

Wow, those unruly thoughts would get her into trouble. Instead, she returned his smile as she stood and walked toward him.

"Hey, I thought I might have to knock on the door and beg you to come out."

She leaned her head to one side. "Why's that?"

"I know I make you nervous."

"You don't make me nervous." That was the biggest bald lie she'd ever told. He did make her jittery with awareness. His simple, far-too-short kiss had awakened something in her that she'd never felt before.

"Okay, it's too fine a day to fight. Friends?" He stuck out his hand.

China took it. His fingers wrapped around hers, strong and confident, as if cocooning them. She mentally shook her head. *Quit the dreamy teenage girl stuff and get with the program.*

She tugged her hand free. "Friends." She looked at his car then back at him. "I think we should take my car. Yours is too perfect and you'll not want to get dirt in it. I have mine set up to transport plants."

"Okay, if you think I can get into it," he said, in the most agreeable tone. "You're the boss."

He went up a notch in her estimation. It was her experience that men want a woman to do as they asked. Her father certainly believed that and the men she'd dated had wanted her to be agreeable all the time. She pursed her lips and cocked her head in question.

"What?" he asked, in complete innocence. Maybe he was sincere.

"I would have thought you'd fight me about going in my car."

"Why? You're the leader of this outing, and I bow to your knowledge."

She laughed and he joined her. For one of the few times in her life she felt carefree. It was nice, very nice.

"Okay, since you're up for Mr. Congeniality then I guess you don't mind me driving either."

"Not at all."

That's right. He'd let Robin drive his car. It had surprised her at the time. Her father always did the driving. Woman couldn't do as good a job, he'd say. Payton seemed perfectly content with the idea. They walked toward her car, which was parked along the street. "When I first met you I took you for one of those males who thought a woman should be two steps behind him."

He grinned as he opened the passenger door. "Well, you never know what surprises I have in store."

That zing of awareness in her middle grew stronger. Did she want to find out? Yes. But should she?

China left Golden Shores behind and headed up the four-lane highway northward. Payton hadn't said much, seemingly glad to sit back and be chauffeured. He been raised with a cook, did he have a chauffeur too? He smelled wonderful, sort of like warm earth.

"So where're we going?" he finally asked.

"To a nursery about ten miles from here. They have the hardiest plants around."

At least now she could concentrate on what he was saying instead of how good he smelled. She'd never be able to get into her car again without thinking of him. She groaned. His scent was sure to linger for a long time.

"You're really into plants, aren't you?" Payton rather liked the way China's eyes lit up when she spoke of going to the nursery. What would it be like to have China's eyes shine in anticipation of seeing him? Somehow the challenge and the idea that it could happen gave him a rush he'd not experienced in a long time.

"Yeah, I'm really into plants."

"Why?"

She jerked her head toward him. Her look was one of shock, as if he'd discovered something he wasn't supposed to see. What was she hiding?

"I starting gardening as a preteen with a neighbor and it grew from there. Pardon the pun." She gave him a smile. "I like growing flowers and that turned into growing tomatoes, and then a full garden patch."

"Interesting."

"What do you mean by that?"

"Just that it's interesting that you turned into a gardener at such a young age."

"I didn't know there was an age limit."

"I'm just making an observation." Time to change the subject, which obviously had an agenda behind it. "Tell me about your name. Where did it come from?"

"My parents."

He smirked. "Funny. How did your parents decide on the name?"

"My father said I looked like a china doll. So there you have it."

"It makes me think of something fragile," Payton said.

"Don't be mistaken by my name. I'm no pushover."

"Believe me, I never thought you were."

"How about the name Payton? It's an interesting name." She made a right turn down a long straight road.

"Oh, I'm from a long line of Paytons. Father, grandfather, great-grandfather, etcetera, etcetera."

"Sounds impressive."

"Yeah. There are some that think so."

She glanced at him. "Not you?"

"I'm proud of the heritage but there is also baggage and pressure that goes with it that I'm not a fan of."

"Oh, poor little rich boy."

He made a scoffing noise. "Not funny."

"Then don't you mean expectations instead of baggage and pressure?"

How had China managed to read between the lines so clearly? He couldn't seem to get his parents to understand why he'd had to get away. Why he had to find his place in the world. Janice certainly wouldn't understand. His name and position had been what had drawn her to him in the first place. It hadn't been true love. The type that stayed with you through thick and thin, in health and adversity. After his illness he had to know that someone wanted him for himself and not his family name.

"Yeah. Expectations."

"I know about those too," she said, so softly that he almost missed the words. "Okay, here's the nursery."

China drove into the packed sand lot and parked. Payton grinned as he stepped out of the car. She was already picking out a child's red wagon that sat among six near the door of a long half-moon shaped building with black netting covering it.

"You pull and I'll pick." China lifted the handle, indicating it. "I'm sorry. I didn't mean to sound like I was ordering you."

"I don't mind taking orders." The smile she gave him

was one of relief. Where had she gotten the idea that she wasn't allowed to speak her mind? He took the wagon handle. "What's this for?"

"To put the plants in." She left off the "dummy" her tone had implied and headed off through the door, leaving him to follow. Payton couldn't remember feeling more out of his element. He'd never been to a plant nursery or been so completely dismissed by a woman for something as mundane as a plant.

He grinned, looped his fingers through the hole of the handle and went after her. This was one more of those new experiences he'd hoped for. He seemed to have a number of them when he was with China. They started down the rows of tables filled with green plants and then up the one with flowering plants. They all looked the same to him.

As they went China's cheeks took on a rosy hue in the heat.

She stopped and looked at him. "I have some suggestions, but do you know anything you might want?"

He was clueless but he'd never admit it. "I'll trust your judgment." And he found that he did.

Payton watched has China moved though the sea of plants in an almost butterfly method. She flitted from one plant to the next, picking up this one and putting it on the wagon, discarding the next and moving on down the line. In no time the wagon was full and she was leading them to the door.

Falling behind, he called, "Hey, is this like going to war? Where you can't speak in case the enemy might hear us?"

She stopped and looked back at him. "What?" Her look implied that she'd almost forgotten he was there. He didn't like that idea at all.

Stepping closer, into her personal space, he asked, "Remember me?"

She blinked, her eyes going wide. Good, at least she knew he was alive.

China stepped away. Payton had been too close. Near enough for her to smell his warm masculine scent with a hint of spice.

"Of course I know you're here." She went back to looking at the plants. "I don't see any Crotons or Hawaiian ti so I need to ask. It would be perfect in the living area and any rooms that face the same direction."

"Like my bedroom."

Payton might not have intended the words to come out gravelly and suggestive but they sounded that way to her.

His bedroom. What was it like? As beautifully decorated as the rest of his home or had he put his own stamp on the space? She didn't think she'd ever know. That was one place she didn't plan to explore.

"We have to find the plants that can handle the direct light. If they don't have them here we can go to another nursery that I know of, if you have time."

"I've got all the time in the world." He acted as if he was perfectly content to do whatever she asked until an unsure expression covered his face for a second. He quickly smiled again. Had he been thinking about having cancer and how close to death he'd been?

"I'll pull these to the checkout counter while you find someone to ask about the others."

A few minutes later China joined him. She was here with Payton. That thought gave her a warm glow. "They don't have what I'm looking for."

"Then off to the next place we go."

"It's about a half an hour up the road," China said as she pulled out of the parking lot.

They road in silence for a while before Payton asked, "Have you lived in this area all your life?"

"Born and bred here."

"Ever thought of moving?" Payton asked.

"Not really. My parents are here. My sister also."

"I have a sister too."

"Really? You close?"

"We were at one time. At least, until I moved down here."

China waited on a car so she could make a left turn. "My sister and I went two different directions a long time ago."

"Why's that?" Payton asked. She didn't have to look at him to know he was studying her profile.

"When my brother ran away at sixteen it changed everything." Why had she told him that? That was one subject she didn't discuss with anyone and certainly not with someone who was almost a stranger.

"What happened?"

"It's too long and too ugly story to go into now." With relief she saw the nursery sign. "Anyway, we're here. We won't be long. If they don't have what I'm looking for then I'll look for it online."

The nursery had one of the types of plants China was searching for. As she was talking to a salesperson Payton wandered over to some brightly painted Italian motif pots. "What about getting a few of these to put some of the plants in?" He picked up a medium-sized one.

China had to admit he had great taste. The pots would be perfect, incorporating all the colors in his home.

"They're rather expensive for the number we need."

He raised a brow. "I think I can handle it."

China didn't doubt that he could.

"How many should we get?"

China kind of liked the sound of *we*. There was some hint of permanence in the word. As if Payton would be around for a while. Payton was making all the noises of someone who could be counted on. He certainly acted like it where his house was concerned. Could she do the same? She wanted to and that was the first step.

She added up the number of Crotons and Hawaiian tis she'd decided he needed. "Eight should be enough. We can come back if we need more."

He pulled a neglected cart over and started placing pots on it. "What do you think about this one?" Payton lifted up a yellow pot, unlike the rest.

"I like it. Do you have a yellow room?"

"I do now," he said with a grin.

When he'd gone through and picked out all he wanted Payton grinned at her and said, like a cute little boy who had just gotten his way, "You know, I like shopping with you. I might do it more often."

She laughed. "But remember I don't do grocery stores."

"Maybe what we need to do is make a deal that I do the grocery shopping and you do everything else. With me tagging along, of course."

"That just might be a plan." Especially as it sounded like a relationship. Were they slipping into one despite her efforts not to?

"Great. Let's get this paid for and get back. I'm beginning to get into this plant stuff."

Fifteen minutes later they were headed down the road. When they passed the sign to the ferry Payton said, "Is that the ferry that comes in at the end of West Beach Road?"

"Yes."

"Do you get seasick?"

"No."

"Then why don't we take the ferry back?" Payton asked.

She didn't want to, but she couldn't tell him the reason. "Okay."

Forty-five minutes later they were waiting in line when the ferry rolled and frothed the water as it docked.

"I can't remember the last time I rode a ferry. Maybe as a child but I'm not even sure I did it then," Payton said.

China couldn't help but smile. He sounded like he was really looking forward to the ride. "I've not ridden it in a long, long time."

Slowly she drove cross the ramp onto the ferry, pulled to the spot the crew member indicated and turned off the engine. Another crew member came to the window for the fare. Before China could get her purse, Payton handed the man money.

When the man had gone she said, "I could have gotten that."

"Don't be unreasonable. You drove your car and you're helping me out so the least I can do is pay the fare." Payton opened the door. "Come on, let's get out and watch."

China reluctantly followed him up the stairs to the observation deck. "I haven't been up here in years."

"Why not?"

Now she was sorry she'd brought it up. "I don't know."

He looked at her. "Give. There's more to it than that. I can tell by the tone of your voice."

"Hey, you don't know anything about the tone of my voice." She took a step away from him.

"I know it gets high when you're aggravated with me, soft and gentle when you are caring for a child and hard as nails when you believe you're right. But all that's beside the point. So answer my question."

He wouldn't let it go so she had to say something. "This was Chad's favorite thing to do."

"Chad?"

"My brother." She looked at the horizon, where the sky was darkening then back to the white-capped water. "Yes."

"Why did he leave?"

"He'd gotten in trouble with the law. Father gave him an ultimatum: follow his rules or get out. The next morning he was gone."

She looked at Payton and found him studying her with eyes that were shadowy with compassion. "Have you heard from him since?"

"No. And I miss him every day." She shivered from memories and from the wind picking up.

Payton stepped closer and put an arm lightly across her shoulders. "Why don't we just pretend this is a first for both of us?"

China felt warmed. He was referring to the ferry ride but, still, the statement sounded more intimate then it should have. She glanced at Payton. He was looking off into the distance.

"Do you ever see dolphins here?" he asked.

"I have seen them. A storm is coming in so they might not be around."

They stood side by side, looking out over the water, barely touching. Somehow the pain of the ugly memories she'd experienced when she'd driven onto the ferry were being replaced by the pleasure of spending time doing something as simple as looking for dolphins.

"Hey, isn't that one?" Payton let go of her and leaned over the rail.

China grabbed his arm. "Don't get too excited. You might go over. Show me where."

Payton stretched his arm outward and she followed the direction he pointed. Seconds later she saw the fin and a glimpse of a silver back coming out of the water.

"There they are again," Payton said with wonder in his voice.

"Yes. Aren't they beautiful?"

"Yes. Beautiful."

His breath whispered across her cheek. She glanced at

him to find him watching her. The sun was covered by clouds, but her cheeks were warm, as if it were high in the sky on the brightest of days.

The grinding roar of the engines going into reverse broke the moment. They were coming in to dock.

"We'd better get in the car or we'll have people honking at us," Payton said, taking her hand and helping her down the metal stairs. They ran to the car, laughing, and climbed in. China started the car just in time to take her place in line.

As they bumped over the docking plate Payton said, "We need to do this again soon."

China couldn't disagree.

CHAPTER SIX

IN THE LAST HOUR, Payton had unloaded plants and pots, hauled them up the stairs and helped China place flowers in hanging baskets and containers. He'd had about enough of greenery but China seemed more than happy to continue.

She was a dynamo where plants were concerned. She'd dove headlong into plotting and placing the greenery as soon as they'd arrived at his house. Now she was busy arranging flowers in the living room. The baskets for the porches would have to wait until he bought hooks to hang them from.

Payton washed his hands in the kitchen sink, which had been a no-no when he'd been growing up. Taking two glasses from the cabinet then adding ice and pouring tea into them, he carried them to the living room. Sweet iced tea was one of a number of things he was quickly learning to love about living in the south.

"China, leave those and come watch the storm with me."

"What?" She looked at him in surprise.

"I like a good storm. Come watch it with me."

"It sounds like a good way to get electrocuted. The storms down here are nothing like the ones you're used to."

"We have plenty of terrible weather in Chicago. Remember it's flat there also. Come on. That can wait. If I have learned anything in the last year it's that stuff can wait."

China looked up from where she knelton the floor and gave him a long searching look. She rose slowly. "Let me wash my hands and I'll meet you outside."

Payton nodded and strolled toward one of the doors to the front porch. Minutes later China stepped out and hesitated. Her gaze moved from him to the dark sky off to the west. She was beautiful with her hair blowing around her face and her chin raised against the wind. This was a formable woman who could stand against a storm in life. He'd never seen that in Janice but he had seen it in his mom when she'd so fearlessly cared for him when he'd been at his worst. China had that same backbone.

She moved to take the chair nearby. Payton patted the extra spot next to him on the love seat. "You can see better from here." After a moment she took the spot he'd indicated but acted as if she was making sure she didn't touch him. He propped his feet up on the low table in front of them and ran an arm across the back of the settee. China sat forward stiffly.

"Relax, I'm not going to bite, and the storm isn't going to be that bad."

The wind grew and whirled around them, whistling around the corners of the house.

"I think I'd better go." China moved to stand.

Payton lightly placed his hand on her shoulder. "You can't. I need a ride to your house to pick up my car, and I'm not ready to go."

He had her there. China's nature wouldn't let her leave him without transportation. She had to always be taking care of someone. This time he rather liked being the focus of her attention and he was going to make the most of it.

"Lean back and watch. Haven't you ever watched a storm coming?"

"Not really." She shifted toward him slightly.

He removed his hand from her shoulder, placing it on the back of the settee.

"Have you always been a thrill-seeker?"

"What do you mean?" He was truly puzzled by her question.

"You wanted to learn to skimboard, the fast sports car, moving so far away from home." She waved a hand around. "Sitting out in the middle of a storm."

"I just want to experience new things. I've never had the time or inclination to just watch a storm come in. I thought it would be fun."

China looked at him closely for another few seconds. The desire to kiss her, take her, shot through him like the bolt of lightning flashing in the dark clouds just offshore. But he didn't. If he acted on his desire he might want more. He'd already made up his mind that friendship was all he could handle. Plus, they'd had a great day and he wasn't about to ruin it.

"Check out the lightning," he said softly, knowing she couldn't resist the suggestion.

As she became enthralled with the show before them, she shifted toward him and leaned back. Payton was tempted to gather her into his arms but he held fast. Watching the storm was building one in him.

When a fat drop of rain landed on China's cheek she squealed. Payton laughed. A full-bodied sound that came from deep in his gut with an "everything right with the world" quality. He'd never laughed when he'd been with Janice.

"I'm not getting wet!" China moved to stand.

Payton pulled her back. "You can't miss the best part. Stay here and I'll be back in a sec." He went into the house and retrieved a largest beach towel from the bath. Returning, he said, "Here, cover up with this."

Taking the towel, China pulled it over her so that it covered her front like a blanket. Payton took his seat again. She lifted a corner of the towel, offering him a place under it. Payton couldn't care less if he got wet, but he wouldn't pass up an opportunity to snuggle with China. Not for all the gold lost in a Spanish galleon during a Caribbean storm. When the towel didn't quite cover one of his legs she moved in closer, giving him more of the material. The rain blew in earnest but they remained dry and warm.

China glanced at him during the angriest part of the storm. "You know, this is rather fun."

"I thought you might like it." He hugged her to him.

Soon the sky was cloudless again, and the only noise came from the water dropping off the eaves. A few silent moments went by before Payton whispered, "This is the best part. Take a deep breath through your nose."

They did so in unison.

"So what do you smell?" he asked.

"Freshness, salt, the scent of the sea grass."

"I smell life," he said softly.

China removed the towel, turned enough that she could meet his gaze "Why, Dr. Jenkins, I do believe you're a closet poet. Thanks for insisting I stay."

"You're welcome. Now I think it's time you take me to my car."

China blinked as if amazed by his remark. She sat up quickly. "Uh, yeah, it's time for me to go. I mean us to go." She headed along the porch toward the stairs. "I'll just wait for you in the car."

China sat staring out the windshield at the newel post of Payton's staircase. What had she been thinking to become moony-eyed over Payton? She'd almost kissed him on the cheek despite her desire to find his lips. She wasn't that forward. They'd shared a pleasant afternoon, and she'd almost ruined it by making a fool of herself. Heck, she wasn't sure how it had happened but she was beginning to like the good doc.

They really had nothing in common. He lived in this big house. She lived in a tiny apartment she didn't own. He had a car that people looked at when he passed. Hers blended in with all the others in the parking lot. He was all about skimboarding and sailing and she favored plants. They only shared medicine. And kisses. Those they unquestionably had in common.

Payton joined her minutes later. They spoke little during the short ride to her house.

As she pulled into the drive he said, "I appreciate your help today. The plants look great. Now all I have to do is not kill them."

"Just water as the little tabs direct and you'll be okay. I'm sorry I didn't think about getting hooks so we could hang the baskets."

"Not your fault. I didn't think about them either. I'll pick some up tomorrow after work. You want to come out and help me hang them?"

China shook her head. "Sorry, I have to take my mom to the doctor. Don't forget that larger pot in your bedroom. It likes that particular type of light."

She'd already spent too much time with him. He was addictive. The hour spent at his house had her rattled. She needed to think, put some space between them. Was he always as wonderful as he had been this afternoon, or would he turn into one of those men who had to have control when you got to really know them?

"Yes, ma'am." He smiled. "Look, now you've got me doing it."

She laughed. "You're becoming a true southerner."

"I guess I am." He touched her arm. "Thanks for your help today. I really enjoyed my afternoon."

"You're welcome."

China turned off the engine and they both climbed out of the car.

"Well, I guess I'll see you tomorrow."

"I'll be there. Good evening, Payton." China headed toward her apartment. She felt his gaze on her as she climbed the steps to her door. Would these conflicting feelings for Payton still be there in the morning? She was afraid they would be. She was already counting the hours until she saw him again.

At the clinic on Saturday morning, just before lunch Payton asked, "China, would you come in my office for a minute, please?"

What was going on? They had been cordial with each other since getting to work, but she'd seen to it that they were never alone. Not that she didn't trust him, it was more like she couldn't trust herself. She'd stayed up far too late into the night thinking about Payton, looking forward to coming to work so she could see him. She didn't like it.

Payton headed toward his office, and she followed slowly. She entered to find him waiting beside his desk. He said, "If you don't mind, would you close the door?"

She started to say that, yes, she minded, but Payton would never embarrass her or do anything she wasn't in agreement with. "Okay." She pushed the door until it made a soft click. "Is something wrong? Are you feeling sick again?"

"No, I'm fine." There was a harsh edge to his tone.

She straightened. "All right, then. So what did you drag me in here for?"

"I asked you, I didn't pull you in here by your hair."

"Look—"

Payton put a hand out, palm up. "Let's not fight. That's not why I ask you in here." He ran the hand through his short hair, mussing it.

China hadn't seen him this unsure before, not even when he'd admitted he'd had cancer. What was going on?

"I think I've bitten off more than I can chew."

She grinned. He'd been using more casual sayings over the last couple of days.

"I'm not sure I can handle the dinner tonight by myself. I've cooked for two but never six. I know this is a lot to ask, and I know how you feel about cooking, but I have no one else to turn to. Would you come early and help me?"

He'd said the words so fast that China had to think about what he'd asked. She wasn't sure how she felt about the statement. Despite her better judgment and her vow to keep space between them, she didn't have the heart to turn him down. "I'll go home and change, and be there as soon as I can."

His smile of relief made her middle flutter.

"Thanks so much, China. I owe you big time. I've already done the shopping so you don't have to worry about helping with that. Now we'd better get back to the patients."

His abrupt end to their conversation somehow disappointed her. Had she expected him to express his undying gratitude by kissing her? That was more like wishful thinking.

Hours later China knocked on the kitchen door to Payton's house. At the faint sound of "Come in," she opened the door.

All she could see of Payton was his backside encased in navy knit running shorts. She had to admit he had a fine behind. Seconds later his head came out from inside the cabinet. Standing, he grinned at her and placed a large boiling pot on the counter. "Hey, there. I was hunting a pan."

"Well, I hope so, otherwise putting you head inside a cabinet would be rather strange."

"You wouldn't be surprised, though, would you?"

"In order not to start an argument I'm going to take the high road and not answer that."

Payton raised his head heavenward. "Thank you for small miracles."

China couldn't help but laugh, something she found that she was doing more often around Payton. When she'd first met him she'd never have guessed they would ever be friends. She could work with anyone but to her great surprise she like spending her off time with him as well.

"I'm a little behind. Would you mind being my second-in-command and chop up the onions and potatoes?"

"I need a knife. What're we having?"

"A beef loin in puff pastry with braised potatoes, salad and a fruit trifle."

"Wow. That sounds wonderful. No seafood?"

"I thought everyone probably got all of that they wanted any time. I wanted to do something different. Besides, it's my specialty." He pulled a bowl out of an upper cabinet.

"So you've made it before."

He handed her a knife. "A number of times."

She put her hands on her hips and glared at him. "So you got me here on false pretenses."

Payton looked directly at her. "Well, yes and no. I can use the help and I find that I rather like spending time with you," he said matter-of-factly.

China's heart thumped against her chest wall. All she could do was stare at him. "Uh, where's a cutting board?"

"It's under the cabinet to the left."

She turned her back to him to go after the board.

"One thing I've learned is that time is precious and I'm not going to waste any more of it. I think you like me also. Or at least your kiss said you do."

China reached for the cutting board and when she turned around Payton was already concentrating on the meat he was preparing. "The potatoes and onions are in the pantry." He nodded toward a door.

Payton had turned all business. Had he really said what she thought he'd said? She found the vegetables and brought them to the island.

"Come and work over here in front of me. There's plenty of room. Next to the windows and porches, I like this kitchen best. It's made for cooking together and entertaining."

"It's wonderful. Nothing like the small one I grew up cooking in."

"When did you start cooking?"

"When I was twelve."

"I came to it much later in life. Ruth, our cook, thought I needed to know something about preparing a meal before I left for college. So I hung out in the kitchen and fell in love with cooking."

"I might have enjoyed it more if I hadn't seen it as a chore."

"Why is that?"

"Just that I had to help out at home."

"I'm not surprised."

"What does that mean?"

"Just typical for you. Helping out."

She stopped chopping and looked at him. "You didn't say that like it's a compliment."

"Don't get mad. It's just an observation."

"I suggest that you keep your observations to yourself

unless you have something nice to say." She made a cut into a potato with more force than required.

"You have the most beautiful brown eyes I've ever seen."

China felt the heat flow up her neck to her cheeks. Her heart fluttered. Never in a million years would she have dreamed that Payton Jenkins would ever flirt with her. Somehow it was empowering.

Payton grinned but kept his head down and pretended to be concentrating on wrapping the loin in pastry. He'd gotten China's attention with his remark about her eyes. They worked together in silence for a while but he was aware of every movement she made.

She was aware of him too. He dropped a knife and she jumped. Tension as deep as the gulf filled the room, and he was enjoying having her a little off center. China put up such a wall where he was concerned that it was nice to see he was making a chink in it. He wasn't sure what the future held for him or if he had the right to be involved with anyone, but where China was concerned he couldn't help himself. She intrigued him.

He slipped the roasting pan into the oven. "Are those potatoes and onions ready?"

"I have one more to cut."

"Great. I'll get them started and then we can set the table. I've already made the trifle and have it in the refrigerator. After we finish the table I'll change and then we can put together the salad."

She nodded and a minute later said, "I'm done. Hand me the pan and I'll put these in it."

He did as she requested. With the same efficiency he admired in her nursing, China cleaned the area and washed her hands.

"Okay, where are the plates, silverware and napkins?"

"I'll get the plates. The silverware is in the drawer to the right of the sink, the napkins in the third drawer down."

Payton was putting the plates on the table when China said with amazement in her voice, "These are all cloth napkins."

"Yes. So?"

She turned and looked at him. "That's all you have?"

"It is. Bring the green ones."

She reached in the drawer and counted to make sure she had all that were required. "I've never known someone who only uses cloth napkins."

"You make it sound like a crime. We only used cloth at my house when I was growing up."

"Yeah, and we only used paper. If my parents own cloth ones, I've never seen them." China brought the napkins and a handful of silverware to the table.

"Well, enjoy using mine tonight."

"I think I will."

Payton glanced at the clock on the wall. "If you don't mind finishing up here, I'm going to take a quick shower and change."

"I'll finish. Do you want to use the regular glasses or do you have something else in mind?"

Payton stopped at the doorway to the living room. "Those are fine. There are some wineglasses up there also." He pointed in the direction of a cabinet she'd not looked in before.

China started placing the silverware around the plates.

"Hey, China."

She looked at him.

"Thanks for your help. Really."

She smiled. "You're welcome."

Payton pulled his shirt up over his head as he went down the hall with a smile on his face. Maybe the being friends idea was overrated. It was fun to tease China. Nice kissing her too and he wanted to do it again. He was starting over in life so why not have some fun? No one said their time together had to last forever.

With the table set and wineglasses waiting, China went outside to check the plants. Payton had hung the orange lantana around the porches. It contrasted well with the yellow of the house and looked beautiful. Any home always felt more comfortable with plants around, or at least she believed so. After checking the dampness of the soil in a couple of baskets, China returned to the living room to look at a pot there. The faint sound of water running told her Payton was still taking a shower.

A buzz from the kitchen drew her attention. She went to see what it was for. Turning the timer off on the oven, she opened the door and checked the loin. Not sure what to do and not wanting Payton's meal to be ruined, she closed the stove door and turned the oven off.

There was no choice. She was going to have to ask Payton what needed to be done. Bracing and reminding herself she was an adult, she headed toward the sound of water. At his bedroom door she called his name. Hearing no answer, she stepped further into the room. What was she going to do if he stepped out of the bathroom naked? Have a heart attack? That was silly. She saw half-naked bodies all the time in her line of work.

Yeah, but none of those were Payton's.

Squaring her shoulders, she walked across the room and knocked firmly on the open bathroom door. "Payton."

That heart attack might not be such a far-fetched idea. Payton's walk-in shower was made of clear glass blocks. She could make out the shape of his body on the other side. He had his hands raised as if he was rinsing his hair. The fleeting idea that she should avert her gaze crossed her mind but her eyes wouldn't cooperate.

"Yeah?"

"Sorry to bother you but the buzzer went off, and I was wondering if I need to take the loin out."

"And I was hoping you had come in to join me."

"In your dreams."

China watched as his silhouette moved to the end of the blocks. Was he going to stand there naked in front of her? Would she look away? Not likely.

Instead, he stuck his head around the edge of the wall. His gaze held hers. "You are."

"Come on, Payton, stop teasing me and tell me what to do about the meat. I should just let the meal get ruined."

He grinned. "You're much too nice a person to do that. Pull it out, please. It needs to rest for ten minutes."

Without another word, China headed back to the kitchen. She searched for the hot pads. Her hands trembled at her first try at taking the heavy pan out. Payton had rattled her. She didn't like it. Control was something she usually managed to maintain, had needed to keep a tight grip on since her brother had left. Someone had to. China took a deep breath and tried again, successfully. This time she sat the pan on the granite counter top with a thump.

Done, she looked up to find Payton standing behind her. She hadn't seen him enter the kitchen but she known he was there just the same. The fresh smell of soap and something that was Payton's alone circled around her.

He leaned over her shoulder to study the golden brown pastry. "Mmm, looks and smells perfect."

She couldn't disagree. "It does look amazing. Impressive, in fact."

He stepped around her and pulled out a basting spoon from a drawer. She'd moved but she'd had to touch him to do so. That she refused to do.

Payton only wore a pair of buff-colored slacks, no shirt

and no shoes. A towel hung around his neck. She'd never been more aware of a man in her life.

He dipped the spoon into the juice at the bottom of the pan and brought it to his lips. She watched as his tongue reached out for the fluid. "Perfect," he breathed. "Want a taste?"

She knew he was talking about the liquid but her focus was on his lips.

"China," he said in a soft, rusty voice, "stop looking at me that way. I don't think you want all the staff at the clinic to find us sprawled across the kitchen counter. Which is going to happen in about three seconds if you don't stop."

She blinked and pushed back, which made her brush his bare chest. The sound of the spoon dropping to the pan came just before Payton's hand caught her upper arm and pulled her gently back toward him.

"Let's see if what we were both thinking is true," he whispered just before his lips met hers, gently at first. But he soon pressed deeper. Payton tasted of beef and salt. His lips requested and promised something wonderful at the same time.

China stepped closer, bringing her hands up to Payton's waist in the hope that there she'd find a way to steady herself. She opened her mouth and Payton accepted the invitation. She wrapped her hands more tightly around his waist, enjoying the warmth of his skin. His arms held her securely. He entered and retreated and entered her mouth again. Heat and desire rose in her until she was sure the earth had tipped out of orbit.

Bit by bit her hands ran across the planes of his back as Payton deepened the kiss.

At the sound of the doorbell chiming, China jerked away and out of his hold. "I'll get that while you dress."

Payton chuckled. "Saved by the bell. This time. China,

don't think for one minute this is over. I will kiss you again. That's a promise." He headed toward his bedroom.

"Not if I don't want you to."

Payton stopped, turned and looked at her before he said, "But you do." Just as abruptly he turned again and walked off.

She groaned. Heaven help her, he was right. She did want him to kiss her again. But she wouldn't let him.

CHAPTER SEVEN

PAYTON WAS PLEASED that his dinner party was turning out to be such a success. Doris and Jean had arrived together. Both had given China suspicious looks when he'd stepped into the room fresh from the shower. Neither woman said anything but he could tell that China was uncomfortable about what they might be thinking. To ease her worries he came right out and said, "I asked China to come early and help me with the preparations. She was a great help."

He winked at China. Her cheeks turned rosy.

By the time Robin and Luke arrived and then Larry and his wife, the party was in full swing. He couldn't remember attending a more boisterous and loud social gathering outside the frat parties he'd gone to in college.

When Doris and then Jean asked if they could see his place, he took everyone on a tour. He noticed that China brought up the rear when they changed rooms. It wasn't until the group reached his bedroom that she stepped out of the crowd. She went over to the Hawaiian ti, which he'd placed close to the window. She lovingly touched a leaf before looking at him.

He smiled and she returned it with warmth in her eyes. It was as if they were sharing a special secret. Somehow it made him stand taller. As if making China happy made him happy.

"Man, you have a beautiful view," Larry's wife remarked.

"Yes, I do." He was looking at China instead of out the window.

"Okay, enough of this girly stuff. Let's eat. I'm starving," Luke stated.

"I have to get things on the table," Payton said. He'd finished the salad and potatoes while China, Doris and Jean had enjoyed the view from the porch. China had offered to help but he'd declined it.

She assisted him placing the food on the table after he'd called that dinner was ready. The conversation during dinner was lively and everyone was complimentary about his culinary skills. A couple of times he looked down the table to see China watching him. It hadn't passed his notice that she hadn't chosen to sit beside him. She was on Luke's right and Robin sat to his left.

Over dessert everyone laughed and told bad medical jokes. He watched as China lifted a spoon full of trifle to her mouth. His groin tightened at the thought of kissing those lips again. As if she'd sensed his interest, she glanced at him as she pulled the spoon from her mouth. Was she teasing him or enjoying the trifle? Either way, he was turned on. That was something he'd not been in some time. It felt good to lust after a woman again. And hunger for China he did. More so every day.

Near eleven, Larry pushed back from the table and said, "I hate to be the one to bring this party to an end, but I have to work tomorrow, unlike some others in this room." He looked pointedly at Payton.

"I appreciate that and will think of you while I'm sailing."

Larry stood and smiled at him. "You know, I'm not sure I like you despite your ability to cook."

Payton rose and walked to the front door with Larry and his wife.

"We enjoyed it, man," Larry said, as he shook Payton's hand.

"Glad you did. Come again." Payton meant it. He liked having people around. He'd pushed them away when he'd been sick and had never really appreciated dinner parties even before that.

Doris and Jean came up behind him. "We've got to go too. Thanks for having us."

"Anytime. I'll see you both on Monday."

"I'll see you on Monday too," China said, as she joined them on the way out the door.

"You're not staying to help clean up?" Payton asked in mock surprise.

Before she could answer Robin said, "I can. I'm a great dishwasher. China, would you mind giving Luke a lift home? He rode with me."

At Payton's stricken look China said in a too-cheerful voice, "Not at all."

"Great. Then I'll get started," Robin said, turning toward the kitchen.

"Luke, I'm ready when you are," China called.

"I'll be right there."

China had stepped out on the porch when Payton grabbed her elbow. "Go sailing with me tomorrow," he said, low enough that only she could hear.

"No."

"Why not? Scared?"

"Of what?"

"Being alone with me. Don't trust yourself, do you?" Payton said, close enough to her ear that it might look like he was kissing it.

"I'm not afraid of you," China hissed.

"Then maybe you're afraid you'll jump my bones."

She moved away and said in an indignant voice, "I am not. Where did the let's-be-friends rule go?"

"What're you two talking about?" Luke asked, striding up to them.

"Nothing. Come on, it's been a long day." China started down the stairs. Luke shrugged as he went by Payton and followed China.

If he let her leave without her agreeing to go sailing there would be no way to convince her over the phone. He had to get her agreement in person. "Hey, China, wait a minute."

She stopped halfway down and turned to look at him. As if Luke was his wing man, he said to China, "I'll wait for you in the car."

Payton stepped down to her. "I've decided rules are made to be broken. I'd really like to take you sailing as a thank-you for your help with the plants and dinner."

"You don't have to." She moved down a step.

"I know you don't, but I do. If you're worried, I'll kiss you again. Then you have my word as a gentleman that I won't." Even in the yellow glow of the porch lights he could see her warring to make a decision. "I promise you'll have good time."

"I'm not much for water sports."

"If you don't enjoy yourself, I'll never ask again."

She took so long to answer he feared she was going to say no. "All right. What time should I be ready?"

"Nine o'clock too early?"

"No." She headed down the steps.

"Bring sunscreen and something to swim in. 'Night, China."

The next morning China again wondered what she had gotten herself into. She couldn't seem to say no to Payton, regardless of how hard she tried. Maybe she just needed to go along and stop fighting him and her feelings. She couldn't remember when she'd last taken time to just enjoy a day, spent it doing nothing constructive.

Before she could talk herself out of going, Payton pulled his car into the drive. The sudden realization that she was going on a date with Payton hit her. This wasn't her helping out a new person in town but them spending personal time together. She didn't date often and she sure didn't date guys like Payton. Her father had her told her more than once to watch out for the smooth-talking, fast-car type of man because they would get her into trouble. She was in over her head—way over.

China swallowed the knot in her throat as she watched Payton walk toward her. Tall, with a tan, he appeared virile and full of life. Dressed in a white collared shirt with his shirttail out, navy shorts and deck shoes, he could be a member of the classic yachting crowd. His broad smile was white against his skin. Payton was breathtaking and so out of her league. What could he possibly see in her?

"Ready?" he asked, reaching down for her beach bag.

She grabbed it, stopping him. "Something has come up. I'm not going to be able to go."

He pinned her with a look, his mouth thinning. "Just this second? Like what?" He snapped his fingers.

"I don't have to tell you."

"Yes, you do. I think that if you break a date with someone they deserve to know the reason. Especially if it's at the last minute."

"I just can't go."

He sat down beside her. "Why, China?"

"Because you and I have nothing in common."

Payton took one of her hands. His thumb ran slowly across the back of her hand as if he was trying to soothe a wild animal. "Oh, I think we had plenty in common last night."

"But that is all we have, sexual attraction."

"So you admit it. You're attracted to me?"

"I think you know I am. I don't go around kissing every man I see." She looked down at her toes, which she'd polished bright pink just minutes before he'd driven up.

"I'm glad to hear that. I had hoped I was special."

"Now you're making fun of me."

"No, I'm not. I'm just trying to find out why all of a sudden you don't want to go sailing with me."

"I just don't see where this is going."

"All this is right now is one friend talking to another and taking that friend sailing to say thank you." Payton caught her gaze. "This is not a NATO pact affecting millions of people. This is two people having fun together and getting to know each other better. Nothing more, nothing less. Go with the flow for once. You might find out you enjoy yourself."

Put that way, her argument sounded rather silly.

"Come on, China. Let's have some fun. I think you take life far too seriously. Enjoy it some. If you don't like sailing I promise to bring you straight in." He put up three fingers. "Scout's honor."

She took a deep breath. "Okay, I can use a day away."

"As far as I'm concerned, you can sunbathe to your heart's content all day long."

"That does sound nice."

Payton stood and helped her to her feet. He didn't let go of her hand as they walked to his car, as if he was afraid she would bolt. Settled in for the ride as they made their way down the East Beach Road to the Golden Shores Marina, China had to admit it was fun having the wind blowing through her hair, the sun on her face and a handsome man at her side. This was what every woman dreamed of. Maybe that was the problem, it seemed too good to be true.

"Were you really a Boy Scout?"

Payton looked at her and grinned. "Eagle Scout, in fact."

"That figures. An overachiever."

"Is that a bad thing?"

"No, I think that's one of the reasons you're such a good doctor."

"My goodness, I'm going to blush. Two compliments in less than an hour. Are you running a fever?" He reached over to briefly touch her forehead.

China slapped his hand away. "Funny doctor. Don't give up your day job to be a comedian." She laughed.

Payton joined her. It was nice to be around someone with a sense of humor. He was right, she was far too serious. Maybe it was time for that to change.

Payton had broken out in a sweat when China had said she wasn't going sailing. For some reason it was important that she come along, see his boat. Friendship was the order of the day. They would spend the day together just getting to know each other better. He loved being on his boat and wanted to share that feeling with China. If she let loose he'd bet she would be a lot of fun. He'd seen hints of if before. A day out on the water might be just the ticket to seeing her less serious side. Problem was that mastering his basic instinct would be the order of the day.

He pulled the car into a parking spot near his slip. Climbing out, Payton grabbed a large brown sack out of the trunk and met China, who had just closed her door. He grinned. "Ready?"

"You really love this sailing stuff, don't you?"

"I do. Nothing like it. I can't believe you've lived here all your life and never been."

"After my brother left, my parents discouraged us from doing anything dangerous. I think they were afraid of losing us."

"I wouldn't consider sailing dangerous. Still, I won't

let anything happen to you. Nothing but fun stuff today."
He took her hand. "Come on, let me show you my baby."

"Baby?"

"Yeah." He gave her hand a tug. "My baby."

They walked down the gray wooden dock.

"This is almost picture perfect. The gleaming white boats against the blue water," China said.

"See, you're already glad you came."

"I guess I am."

"Don't get too excited." He stopped near the end of the dock where his boat bobbed gently in the water.

"*Free at Last*," China read out the gold script letters paint on the transom. "I know little about sailing but I thought a boat was supposed to be named after a woman."

"Some are. Since I don't know a woman to name mine after, I just put how I feel when I'm on her."

China pursed her lips and nodded her head as if she'd learn something significant. "Interesting."

"I'm not sure that's a positive response but maybe you'll understand after you take a ride." Stepping onto the edge of the boat, he held his hand up to help China board.

She placed her hand in his and carefully stepped onto the boat then down onto the deck.

"You can have a seat on that bench. I've got to untie us. I'll be right back."

Payton jumped to the dock and glanced back at China. She sat stiffly on the green cushioned seat with a look of unease marring her features. "Hey." She met his look. "I'm not going to let anything happen to you. I really do think you'll have fun."

"I'm all right."

"Then smile."

She gave him a bright but unconvincing smile. Hurrying to the bow, he released the rope securing the boat to the dock and returned to the stern to do the same. Climbing aboard again, Payton started the small motor and put it into gear. Slowly he maneuvered out of the slip. He glanced back to find China watching with interest as they put distance between them and land. Her body had lost that tense appearance. She was coming around.

China raised her face to the sun, closed her eyes and basked in its warmth. The sound of water lapping against the side of the boat had her drifting off. When was the last time she'd napped?

The sharp snap and flutter of a sail catching the wind brought her eyes wide open. She couldn't see Payton, but sounds of movement in front of the cabin said he was there. The wind whipped her hair into her mouth and she gathered it in one hand and pulled it to the side. She stood, swaying as the boat shifted in the water. Bracing her feet apart and holding on to the edge of the roof of the cabin, she looked over it. Payton was leaning over a winch, winding up rope at a rapid speed.

She had a fine view and time to enjoy it. Payton's muscles flexed with his effort. His legs were strong and sturdy. He was a man in his element, confident and in control. As he straightened and turned to adjust something she was presented an unobstructed view of his firm butt.

Payton turned. His gaze met hers as if he knew she'd been ogling him. A self-assured smile slowly spread across his face as he came toward her. Her lips lifted as if of their own accord. The man had that kind of effect on her.

Looking down on her from the top of the cabin, he said, "Hey, sleepyhead, you'd better sit down. I'm come down to bring the boom around. I wouldn't want you to go swimming without me."

Captivated, China could do nothing but stare at him. With the sun at his back, his hair tousled by the wind and his white smile for her only, she had to remind herself to breathe. It was beyond her wildest dreams that she could be off sailing with such a gorgeous man.

He lithely made his way along the narrow companionway between the side of the boat and the cabin to join her. "China, you okay?"

She blinked and sucked in a breath. "Yeah, why?"

"I've been talking to you, and you've been ignoring me."

The problem was she *hadn't* been ignoring him, she'd been fixated. "What did you say?"

He took her elbow and led her to the bench. "I'm going to let you handle the rudder while I take care of the boom. We need to tack soon so I can show you my favorite new spot."

She shook her head. "I don't know anything about the rudder." China was afraid her apprehension was showing again.

"You don't have to. It's easy and I'm going to show you how." He took her hand and pulled her toward the seat again. "Sit down."

She took the same spot she been in earlier.

"This…" Payton put his hand on the shiny, well cared-for wooden handle that was just behind the seat "…moves the rudder." He demonstrated by pushing it back and forth. The boat shifted to the right and then to the left as he moved the handle. "Now you put your hand right here."

China put her hand where he indicated and Payton placed his palm over it. "Now, all I want you to do it hold it steady."

"I don't think—"

"No thinking required. You'll be fine. Relax and enjoy. I'm letting go now."

Her heart hung in her throat as his fingers left hers.

"See that point of land straight ahead?"

She nodded.

"Keep us headed in that direction. We aren't going to leave the bay so there shouldn't be much more wind than this. I'm going to get the line to the boom." Payton moved to leave her.

"Don't go."

"I'll be right back. You just adjust the rudder back and forth and keep us headed for that point."

Payton disappeared from sight. She looked at her hand to find that the knuckles were turning white. She eased her grip on the wood and took a slow deep breath. Payton wouldn't have left her with his pride and joy if he didn't trust that she could handle it. Finding the point of land again, she moved the rudder and brought the boat in line again. A sense of pride washed through her. She was controlling this huge sailboat. She'd felt out of control so much of her life that it was invigorating to feel some power.

She smiled up at Payton when he returned.

"You're starting to enjoy yourself, aren't you?"

She lifted her chin and let the wind blow in her face. "I have to admit, I'm having fun."

Holding a rope in his hand, Payton came to sit down beside her. "I was hoping you would."

The earnest look he gave her said that it had really mattered to him that she enjoyed sailing. Why?

"Okay, here's the important part and the dangerous one if you don't pay attention and listen. I don't want you to get hurt."

Suddenly the confidence she'd felt ebbed away.

"When I bring the jib around you have to duck. If you don't, the boom with hit you in the head. So when I yell 'Duck', you'd better do it."

Her poise returned. Surely she could do that without any problem.

"You ready?"

"I'm ready."

"Okay, here we go."

* * *

Payton couldn't help but grin at the determination in China's voice. She approached sailing just as she did her nursing and gardening: head on. He found it refreshing. Found her extremely desirable. Would that passion be just as intense in her lovemaking? With every fiber of his being he wanted to find out. To see her come alive beneath him. Why had he ever agreed to make this a friendly trip?

He pulled the rope and the boom began to swing toward them. It gained momentum during the movement. When it was almost parallel with the boat, Payton yelled, "Duck."

They both leaned over, bringing their heads close together. After the boom passed by them, he positioned it and the jib sail caught the wind. The boat jerked and moved swiftly across the water.

He looked at China. She wore a smile from ear to ear. A surge of delight filled him, like none he'd felt since being told he was in remission. China was bewitching him. We're just friends, he had to keep reminding himself. "You're having fun?"

She glanced at him. "This is amazing. I'm so glad you insisted I come."

"I'm glad I did too. You're beautiful."

She stared at him with questioning eyes and parted lips. The desire to kiss her made his chest ache, but he'd promised it would be a sociable day, no pressure. Instead, he laid his hand over hers and adjusted the rudder. "Don't forget we have to head toward that point."

China pulled her hand out from under his and pushed his off the rudder handle. "I've got this."

"Aye, aye, Captain Bligh."

China's laughed intertwined with Payton's. The sound made her chest constrict. She liked sharing something simple as a laugh with him. What would it be like to have that in her life all the time? She was still smiling half an hour later as she ducked on Payton's command as they tacked their way across the bay. She couldn't remember when she'd had more fun.

"Okay, we're going to anchor here. I need a swim." Payton handed her the rope.

"What am going to do with this?"

"Just hold it for a minute. I'm going to unfurl the sails and drop anchor." He climbed around the cabin. Soon the jib sail was coming down and next the mainsail collapsed. The boat began to drift. A few minutes later Payton returned.

"You can let go of the rudder and the rope now," he said in a voice full of mischief.

She placed her hands in her lap. "Are you making fun of me?"

"I would never do that."

"I should hope not." She used her most indignant voice.

Payton reached for the hem of his shirt and pulled it up. "You can change in the cabin if you wish."

"I don't think I'm going to swim."

He stopped midway through removing his shirt and gave her a pointed look. "You do swim, don't you?"

"I do."

"Then why not?"

China could think of any number of answers to that question. *I've not swum in years. I don't want you to see me in a bathing suit. I might jump your bones if I see you in yours.* "I'll just wait for you here," she finally murmured.

He let his shirt drop back into place. "If you don't swim I'm going to throw you in clothes and all."

"You wouldn't dare." She glared at him.

"Do you really want to try me?"

Payton stood above her with his feet braced against the gentle roll of the boat and a determined look on his face. "Well, I guess I'll change."

"Good choice."

Dipping her head to enter the cabin without hitting her head, she stepped into a narrow space with a bunk filling one side with cabinets above and below it. On the other side was a counter with a mini-sink and equally small refrigerator below. At the end of the aisle was a door that must lead to the bath.

The sound of water splashing drifted in. Payton must be in the water. Taking a deep breath, China pulled the far-too-tiny pink pieces of her bikini out of the beach bag. Why hadn't she gone out and bought a one-piece? She didn't wear a bathing suit often. Her two-piece was years old. She liked to sunbathe sometimes so she'd chosen a bikini for that reason, with no intention of wearing it in front of someone like Payton.

Someone like Payton? Someone she was attracted to.

Groaning, she slipped into the suit and was grateful there was no mirror for her to review how she looked. It was best she just get into the water as soon as possible. She braced herself with another deep breath and gathered her towel. Stepping into the sunshine again, she looked out across the expanse of water. She had to admit it was wonderful to be so far away from all responsibilities. There were a few other boats around but they were just dots in the distance. She and Payton were alone.

"Hey, slowpoke. Come on in," Payton called from below her.

She moved to the side so she could see him.

A wolf whistle rent the air. She didn't have to look in the mirror to know that she was as pink as her suit after that sound of appreciation. China glared at him. "Stop." She had to get in the water soon. "Is there a ladder I can use?"

"Just jump. It's plenty deep here."

She dropped her towel and hesitated a moment before

she leapt through the air. Seconds later, she came up, sputtering salt water.

"You're supposed to close your mouth before you hit the water," Payton remarked from where he had his hands wrapped across a plastic float.

"I know that," she barked, as she pushed her hair out of her face and kicked her legs at the same time.

"Come here and share my float. You'll get tired, treading water."

Payton's smile was large and inviting. His damp shoulders glistened in the sunlight. The urge to run her hand over the contracted muscles almost got the better of her. The man was making her crazy. She wasn't sure it was a good idea to get close to Payton when he was fully dressed but barely clothed and wet was clearly a bad idea.

Did she have a choice? She couldn't tread water forever. Slowly, she paddled toward him. He didn't move, making no effort to meet her halfway. When she was close enough to touch the float he shifted to the other end so she had plenty of space and they were in no danger of coming into contact. At least he was keeping his promise not to touch her, kiss her.

She wanted him to. Every fiber of her being screamed for him to do so. If she let go, gave in, what would happen?

Hot sex, a few days, weeks, maybe months of good times, but it would end. It always did. Her family had been fun to be a part of at one time. A family together, and then it had been over. Her family dynamics had taught her that if you messed up you were out. She wasn't going to set herself up for that kind of hurt. She'd do something wrong and Payton wouldn't want her anymore.

A few minutes went by with neither of them saying anything as they drifted along next to the boat. She glanced at Payton and he was looking off toward the shore as if he had no idea she was around. Here she was, half-dressed, and he acted as if she didn't exist. She was so aware of him her body hummed.

What would it be like to touch his water-slick body? Feel those muscles. Be held against him? She needed to get a grip. She couldn't stand the tension that was building like a rogue wave. She had to ease it or she would be swept away.

"I think I'll swim out a little." She didn't wait for Payton's response.

With nice smooth strokes remembered from childhood swimming lessons, she moved away and parallel to the boat. She'd not gone far before she saw Payton keeping up with her stroke for stroke.

She continued on and he did also. When she'd gone as far as she could without resting she stopped. He did too.

"Are you following me?" she asked in a playful tone.

"Yes."

She started back toward the mattress left floating in the water. Payton joined her but remained just out of touching distance. She stopped again.

"Stop following me." She cupped a hand and pushed water toward him. It splashed him in the face.

"So that's the way you want it to be." Payton returned a handful of water.

This time China dared to get closer then sent water flying his way. He returned it. Not to be outdone, she charged him, placing her hands on his shoulders in an effort to push him under.

When she made a move to retreat, Payton captured her wrist and pulled her to him.

"I thought you were going to keep your hands to yourself."

"You touched first. All's fair now."

The heat of his desire pressed firm and erect against her stomach. He hadn't been as immune to her as she'd believed. A hot longing filled her. Payton's hand skimmed more than stroked her as it followed the curvature of her hip over her waist to stop just under her arm. A tiny part of her brain registered that he must be standing on a sand bar. His other hand cupped her behind and held her securely against his length. The thumb of his other hand pushed against the material covering her breast, finding its way underneath. She moaned. Payton's fingers moved out from under her suit to the back and pulled at the strings holding it secure, leaving her top to float around her neck.

"Wrap your legs around my waist."

In a haze of need China did as he requested, bringing herself into a position where his length teased her center.

His voice was husky and low as he demanded, "Hold on to my shoulders and lean back. I want to see you, touch you, taste you."

She came out of the passion-filled daze long enough to say, "I don't think—"

"Sweetheart, it's only you and me for miles. Look at me."

Her gaze came up to lock with his. His eyes were dark with need, and looked like the stormclouds they'd watched roll in days earlier.

China's heart skipped a beat. It was a heady feeling to know she'd put that look in his eyes. She did as he asked. Titillated, excitement flowed through her veins. Hypersensitive to every movement of Payton's hands across her belly, over her ribs until they cupped her breast, she shivered.

His dark head slowly descended. She held her breath as his tongue flicked her straining nipple. China moaned. Her core tightened as heat coiled in her. She shifted against him. Payton made a throaty sound of passion. She'd never before felt such blistering, intense need. Allowing her no time to adsorb what was happening, he brought his lips down to her breast again and sucked. Her hips flexed, pushing her core against him.

Payton groaned as if in pain but his focus didn't leave her

breast. His wet tongue circled her nipple and China moved forward again. His mouth released her and he mumbled between fleeting kisses across her chest, "Sweetheart, you're killing me," before his mouth captured her other nipple.

China's fingers bored into his shoulders, clinging for dear life in the middle of the emotional storm Payton was creating within her.

She wanted, wanted… She wanted Payton. Forget all her "should nots." She had to have him.

His hand slid along her back and between her shoulders to cup the back of her head. He brought her mouth forward to meet his lips.

The kiss was one of reassurance. Deep, slow and searing.

The heat in her exploded into a raging fire.

His other hand lowered, his finger found the edge of her bikini bottom and pushed beneath. China's heart tapped out of control. Instinctively, she loosened her grip on his shoulders, giving his prying hand better access.

He didn't hesitate to take her offering. His fingers circled her thigh until they reached the jointure of her legs. Pushing aside the narrow scrap of material, he teased her center.

The throbbing built until she squirmed. She had to have his touch. Begged for it. He had to stop the ragging need that clawed for release. China flexed her hips in invitation.

Payton softly chuckled as his mouth brushed over her jaw. "Not yet, sweetheart." His dipped his finger into her center but just enough to find the wet warmth that was her and not the Gulf.

When she whimpered in complaint, he reentered as far as he could. With a sigh of rapture, China squeezed her legs around Payton's waist, arched her back and let the sensation of pure, perfect, pleasure overtake her.

CHAPTER EIGHT

PAYTON HAD NEVER seen anything more stunning. He'd traveled all over Europe. Studied the most famous of paintings, visited the Alps in the winter, but noting came close to preparing him for what China looked like with her breasts raised to the sun and coming apart in his arms. He gave thanks that he'd lived to see it. China in her glory was the essence of what being alive meant.

He'd stepped over the line. There was no turning back now. He wanted more. All.

China had touched him and that had been all it had taken to send him over the edge. He'd tried to keep things friendly. Had given her space on the float. Had swum far enough away they wouldn't accidentally brush against each other. Then she'd come after him. He wanted that fire, that passion.

Payton pulled her to him and held her close. He waited until her breathing evened and her legs were no longer circling his waist and dangled in the water. Holding her around the waist, he let her stand. He took her hand. "Can you swim to the boat?"

She didn't answer.

"China, please look at me, sweetheart." She finally lifted her gaze to meet his. "Thank you."

"Why? You didn't…"

"No I didn't. But you were the most wondrous thing I've ever seen. Now, if you think you can swim, I'd like to go back to the boat and spend some more time in private exploring you."

"I can swim."

"Turn around and let me tie your top."

She presented him her back. After he'd fixed her top in place he stepped close enough to let her know that his desire hadn't diminished. He placed a kiss on the ridge of her shoulder.

They walked to the end of the sandbar hand in hand. As the water became too deep, they swam. At the boat, Payton lowered the small ladder at the back and climbed aboard. He took China's hand and helped her to the deck. She started to pull her hand away but he held it fast. He took her into his arms and gave her a soft kiss that should leave her no doubt she was desired.

The subdued and no longer forthright China had him worried that she might be regretting what had happened in the water. He didn't want that. Quite the contrary, he wanted her as hot and bothered as she'd been earlier.

Seconds later her arms came up to circle his neck. Her mouth opened and his tongue intertwined with hers. His manhood pulsated for release between them.

Payton pulled his mouth away. "Sweetheart, it has been a long time for me. I'm not going to last much longer. You deserve better, but could we go inside the cabin where I don't have to worry about sharing you with the world?"

She raised her big doe-like eyes to meet his gaze and nodded slightly. Releasing her, he took her hand and led her into the cabin.

Slow down, man, or you're going to scare her.

Taking a deep breath in the hope of calming his libido, he turned to face China. Her eyes were wide. They held a hint of anticipation mixed with uncertainty. That was one of the many aspects of her personality that he found appealing. She seemed to be confident and sure one minute, needy and naive the next.

Payton cupped her face, brushing his thumb across her cheek. "You're beautiful."

Her gaze left his for a spot somewhere on the bunk.

"Look at me, China." Her look met his again. He said softly, "I don't lie." She blinked as if in acceptance.

Payton ran the pad of his thumb over her kiss-swollen lips and she smiled. It was one of a woman who suddenly grasped her power.

China placed her hands on his chest. With exceedingly slow movements she trailed her fingers over his skin, touching and circling his nipple before moving on follow the ridge of his pectoral muscle. She skimmed her palm across his chest like a gentle wind, making his skin tingle in her wake. Stepping closer, she placed a kiss on his neck and nipped his skin before going up on her toes. She brushed her body against his already straining erection.

Could he take much more? Afraid to touch her for fear he'd push her against the bath door and take her without thought, he kept his hands tightly fisted at his sides, giving her time to feed her need.

As she kissed his jaw her hands traveled down over his ribs to his waist until they reached the top of his swim trunks. There she ran her fingers around the line of his waistband. At the back, China pushed a finger under the material but quickly pull it out again.

He groaned and moved a half a step closer. The woman would be the death of him.

"Not much fun to be teased, is it?" she murmured next to his mouth.

He wasn't answering that question because if he did it wouldn't be with words but actions.

She went flat-footed again and began to explore his chest

with her tongue. One hand left his waist to brush against his manhood.

That did it. In one swift motion he sealed her mouth with his, tongue finding her warm sanctuary as he picked her up, turned around and fell to the bunk.

Payton rolled so that he didn't crush her. China's legs were entangled with his. He ran a hand up the expanse of the creamy silken skin of a thigh until he found the bottom of her bikini. Tugging, and with her help, he removed them. Just as quickly he had her top on the floor. Standing, he pushed his wet bathing suit down. He glanced at China. She'd rolled onto her side with an arm hiding her breasts from view as she unabashedly watched him.

"Like what you see?"

The corners of her lips rose. That small action was enough to make him feel ten feet tall. No longer feeling like a victim of cancer, he found his previous male swagger returning under her admiration.

If she wanted a show he'd give her one. Turning slowly, he presented her with his back as he dug into the backpack he kept hanging on a peg. With relief he found what he sought. Just before he turned around, the touch of a finger moving over one cheek of his backside had his blood heating to boiling.

"I've been wondering what that butt looked like without clothes covering it."

His heart rate went into hyper mode. With a rumble deep in his throat he opened the package and prepared himself. Turning, he came down on her and at the same time pushed her back against the bunk. Nudging her legs apart, he looked at her. China reached for him, pulling him to her as he pushed forward and found her hot, waiting center. She lifted her hips in welcome.

China was so incredibly accepting and responsive to his every touch. He leaned down and kissed her, and to his great satisfaction she shuddered in his arms. He followed with his own release to collapse next to her, one leg resting possessively across one of hers.

While ill, he'd not felt like having sex. Being dumped hadn't helped and he'd never been into mindless encounters. But never had he had such mind-blowing sex.

But that wasn't accurate either. It was lovemaking when shared with China.

China looked at Payton lying beside her. Her head rested on his outstretched arm. She was snuggled close and one of his legs was entwined with hers. Moving would be impossible even if she wanted to, which she didn't.

When she'd met Payton never in a million years would she have believed that she'd end up in his arms. A fleeting touch of lips along her ear said that he was waking. She turned her face into the crook of his neck and inhaled the warm, musky scent of him. No matter how long she lived she'd remember this.

China didn't know if it had happened when she'd called him an idiot and he'd taken it so well, or had it been when they'd watched the storm roll in, but she had let this man charm her, and she liked it.

Payton's hand brushed back her hair from her face. "You okay?"

"Ah-ha."

"You might want to look at me so I know for sure."

China raised her head and smiled. "I'm better than okay."

"I'm sorry things were rushed. I'll do better next time."

More brazen than she'd ever been in her life, China shifted out of his hold and turned so her arms crossed and rested on his chest. "I'm not complaining. I thought you rather excelled at being rushed."

His grin was slow and sexy. "Those kinds of compliments can get you almost anything."

"How about something to eat? I'm starving."

"That I can do." Payton gave her a quick kiss before he stood. "I brought a picnic lunch. Nothing fancy."

"I don't need fancy. Just substantial."

"Here." He handled her a long thin piece of glossy floral fabric that had been hanging from a peg on the wall. "You can put this on while your bathing suit dries."

"I'm not putting on some other woman's sarong, am I?"

"Yes."

"Yes?" she shrieked, throwing her legs over the side of the bunk and grabbing the blanket to cover herself.

Payton grabbed her shoulders, stopping her. "I kind of like you jealous." He placed a swift kiss on her lips. "It's my sister's. She left it here the last time she came sailing with me."

China relaxed.

Payton opened a small cabinet above the bunk, giving China a full view of his physique. The urge to reach out and run her fingers over his tight abdominals had her hand trembling. He had gained some weight over the last few weeks. If she hadn't known he'd been sick she would have never guessed.

He must have sensed she was admiring him. "If you don't stop staring at me like that, you're going to be really hungry by the time we get to food."

China swallowed hard. Was she brave enough to call his bluff? Maybe not a few weeks ago but now... She reached out and let her hand drift over his warm skin. It rippled beneath her touch. She watched in fascination as his manhood grew and stood proudly before her.

Payton growled, dropping the shorts he'd been holding to the floor. "Now you've done it. No food for you."

China didn't mind at all.

Payton laid out on the deck a sheet he'd retrieved from the drawer under the bunk. Of the few supplies he'd brought with him from the house, a tablecloth hadn't been on the list. He set the sack he'd carried aboard in the center.

He'd left the cabin so China could dress and have a few moments to herself. He needed them too. The afternoon had been intense, amazing and totally mind-blowing. China took so long to join him that he worried he might have to go in after her. Maybe giving her some space had been a bad idea. The one thing he didn't want her to do was withdraw. He wasn't ready to let go of what he'd experienced in her arms.

He cared too much about her. But could there really be more? What if he got sick again? Was he willing to put her through that? If he took a chance, would she leave him like Janice had?

"Hey," China said, bringing him out of his dark thoughts. With the sun as a backdrop, she looked sweet, fresh and well loved. His heart swelled. He'd never seen a woman look more desirable. With great restraint, he stopped himself from grabbing her and taking her again.

"Hi." The simple word came out rusty. He cleared his throat. "Come and have some lunch." Payton stood and stepped to meet her. Offering his hand, he was pleased when China took it. He led her around one side of the cabin to the bow of the boat.

Her gasp made him look at her. "Is something wrong?"

"No. This is just so…wonderful. I hadn't any idea you planned to eat up here."

Payton smiled, pleased with his surprise.

She visibly relaxed.

"Come sit down. I think you'll like my other surprise as well."

Payton helped her sit on a cushion and took his place, making a point not to come into contact with her. He was afraid if he did the food would be forgotten one more time.

Opening the brown bag, he pulled out a smaller white one with the name "Sid's" printed in red on the side.

"You stopped by Sid's."

The sound of amazement in her voice made him smile. "I did," he said proudly. He opened the bag, pulled out a sandwich in a wrapper and handed it to her.

"A shrimp po boy. My favorite."

"I know. I asked."

She looked at him with a shocked expression. "What's wrong?"

"It's just that I don't think anyone has ever gone to the trouble to ask what I like."

Why? Hadn't someone, her parents, ever cared enough to be interested in her likes and dislikes? "Well, I did." He grinned. "I also found out that you like hush puppies almost as much as you do chocolate." Payton pulled his sandwich out of the bag then offered China a canned drink from the small, soft-sided cooler he had nearby. He removed the wrapping from his sandwich and took a bite. "This is good." He shook the thick sandwich slightly in the air.

"You didn't think you'd like it?"

He chuckled. "I guess not, but I should've known better." As they ate he looked out over the water. Finishing his sandwich, he remarked, "It must have been nice to live in such an ideal place. Small-town USA. The beach nearby. Everyone knowing what you like to eat."

Had China flinched?

She didn't look at him as she said, "Sometimes things aren't as ideal on the inside as they appear on the outside. Even paradise has its problems."

"That's mighty cynical."

"You never know what towns, families, people are like until you're a part of them."

"My family is pretty tight-knit. Or at least they were until I left. I'm close to my sister, but then again she is about the only one not mad at me. Her husband and kids are great. The tough part about being in a family is that it doesn't go well when you don't go along with the 'family plan.'"

China put her sandwich down on a napkin and looked off into the distance. "I can hardly remember what our family plan was"

"Why's that?" Payton asked softly.

China didn't understand it but for some reason she wanted Payton to know, to tell him the whole story. "I had a solid family. You know, the kind that everyone looks at and says, 'That's the perfect family.' A father who had a good job, a mom who was home for us, three kids and a dog." She put her hand up and made quotations marks in the air. "The perfect American family."

"Something happen to that?"

"My brother turned sixteen and it was as if everything exploded. The band that had held us tight popped off. Chad had always been headstrong but as a teenager he really started bucking the rules. Began running around with the wrong crowd. Or at least it wasn't the crowd my parents wanted him to be involved in."

She paused. Did she really want Payton to know all her dirty laundry?

"And?"

With a sigh of resignation she continued. "Father got wind of it and cracked down. Hard. He suspected Chad was drinking and doing drugs. He had Mom search his room regularly. Dad forbade him to go out at night. Told him who he could see and not see. My brother rebelled big time. Things got difficult at home, his grades dropped and his relationship with Father went from bad to worse. There was screaming all the time, doors slamming. Mom and Father couldn't agree about how to handle Chad and they fought. Mom isn't a strong person and she finally gave up and let Dad have his way." China took a sip of her drink, easing her dry throat.

"When the police called..." she hesitated but then blurted it out "...to say they'd picked up Chad on the beach, smoking pot with a group of other teens, my father went ballistic. Mom tried to calm him down but he wouldn't listen to reason. Chad stayed in jail overnight. Father didn't even drive him home."

"And he ran away."

She nodded, hating to see the look of pity on Payton's face, but as she'd gone this far she might as well tell him everything. She said softly, "Mom and Father blamed each other for Chad's behavior. She said he was too hard on him and he believed she went behind his back and let Chad have his way too much. I don't know which it was. My parents still struggle with not knowing what has happened to him. Everything in our lives became either before or after Chad left. Not that we ever talk about it."

"That had to have been tough."

"Yeah, it was. Still is. Our family came apart like an old rag. Mom and Father are still married but they never really talk. My younger sister doesn't speak to them. She was close to Chad and blames them for pushing him out. I even have to work at it to get her to have anything to do with me. She wanted out of the house and I just wanted what we had before my brother left—my happy family back. Kelsey managed to get through high school without getting into any real trouble. I ran interference most of the time when I thought Father might really blow his top."

"Where's your sister now?"

"Oh, she lives here in town."

"And you don't see her?"

"It does sound bad when you put it like that. I see her at Christmastime mostly. Even then I have to beg her to meet me somewhere. She refuses to go to our parents'. Won't have anything to do with them. I might see her on an occasional birthday. I send cards on hers but she doesn't do that in return. She's a nutritionist at the hospital. There were a few years there I didn't think she would finish school but she did." China looked away from Payton. "I shouldn't have dumped this on you. I'm sure you know more now about my family than you wanted to."

"I'm glad you told me." He brushed his thumb across her hand. "I want to know everything about you."

She gave him a weak smile and removed her hand.

"Have you ever looked for your brother?"

"I think Mom did for a while without Father knowing it but the most I do is check the paper and see if he is ever in it. I think at this point on some level even Father would like to know that he isn't dead. I certainly would." She picked up her sandwich again. "Enough about my life. Hadn't we better be getting back?"

"Are you ready to be captain again?"

"I kind of like being in control."

He gave her a suggestive grin. "I'm going to keep that in mind."

She heat crawl up her neck. "I didn't mean it like that."

He cupped her cheek. "Don't apologize. I rather like the idea. And you're right. We should be thinking about getting back."

Together they gathered up what was left of their meal and stored it below. She changed into her top and jeans before leaving the cabin. Payton was coming in as she was going out. He pulled her to him, taking her mouth in a sweet and tender kiss. China wrapped her arms around his neck and leaned into him. A heavenly minute later Payton broke away with a groan.

"If we don't stop here, I'm going to take you again right out here on the deck when I have a far more comfortable bed at my house."

She gave him a pointed look. "Are you assuming that I'm going to join you?"

"Sweetheart, with you I don't dare assume. The best I can do is hope. You always seem to surprise me." With an exhalation he stepped away. "I'll get the mainsail up," he called. "You want to man the rudder again while I handle the jib?"

It was dusk when China watched as Payton maneuvered the boat into the slip at the marina. She had to admit this had been the best day of her life. Perfect. But could it last? Could he be her safe haven?

She had so much baggage. Payton did too. Did he even want more than a sexual relationship? Could she or would she agree to anything further if he did? She needed security and he had just moved to town, had a new job and was trying to figure out the direction he wanted his life to go. Payton didn't sound like the man for her in the long run.

China studied his profile. Straight backed with wide shoulders, Payton looked as if he'd been born on a boat. His ability to make her come alive when he touched her made her shiver to think about it. China smiled. She really couldn't resist him.

Payton showed her how to tie the boat firmly at the bow and had her do it at the stern, guiding her through the steps. China waited while he hopped aboard again and got their lunch trash. He climbed back onto the dock, tossed the bag in a nearby garbage can, took her hand and they walked toward his car. They passed a group of deep-sea fishing boats along the way. On one, a couple of men looked as if they were working on some fishing gear.

"Have you ever been deep-sea fishing?" Payton asked.

"N—"

The air was suddenly scorched by a four-letter word. They both stopped and looked back.

One of the men was holding his hand up and jumping around.

"Pete, stand still and let me have a look," the other man said in an annoyed voice.

"Wh'ta you need to look for? You're the one who pushed the damn hook through my finger."

"I've got to get it out," the other man said in a high voice.

"You're not touching me. You'd kill me," Pete yelled.

"Then I'll take you to the emergency room."

"That'll cost too much. No insurance."

China and Payton walked over to the boat. "Can we help? I'm Dr. Payton Jenkins and this is China Davis. She's a nurse."

Peter stopped pacing, his face contorted in pain. "Yeah." He held up his meaty finger for them to see. Between the first and second knuckle of his index finger the bright gold eye end of a nook jutted from his skin. There wasn't any blood but the tight white line around Pete's mouth told it was painful.

"You have a first-aid kit?" Payton asked.

"Yeah," the man without the hook in his finger said.

"Get it, please."

"Right away." He disappeared into the cabin of the boat.

The dimming lighting along the pier necessitated that Payton and China climb aboard in order to see. The light of the cabin overhang was better, otherwise she would have insisted that Payton work on the dock. Compared to Payton's immaculate sailboat, this one was a trash dump. He stepped onto the boat then helped her. In short order, which China was astonished by, the man returned with the first-aid kit. Apparently things were more in organized inside the cabin.

"Okay, Pete, you need to sit down." Payton looked around as if unsure where that would happen.

The man pushed the stuff piled on a raised captain's

chair off onto the deck with a clatter. Pete dropped into the chair without question, looking far too pale in the faint light.

With a raised eyebrow of bewilderment that was almost comical Payton said, "All right, then, let's see what we've got." Payton took the man's hand in his and examined the wound site. He looked at Pete. "You know I can't pull this back. The barb will get more securely stuck in your finger. That will require surgery."

"I was 'fraid of that," he said in a tight voice as he glared at his friend.

"I'm going to have to push it though. The one promise I can make is that it's going to hurt like the devil."

"Just do it, Doc. I can't walk around with this." He glanced at China as if reminding himself to watch his language. "Blasted hook in my finger."

"I'm going to need some wire pliers. Got any?"

"Sure," Ralph said. "What kind do you want?"

"The sharpest will suffice."

"Coming up."

Payton turned his attention back to Pete. "I'm going to clip off the eye end of the hook and use that end to push it through." Payton rubbed the spot on the finger where the hook should come through. "The skin on our fingers is some of the toughest of the body. Yours is especially thick because of the type of work you do. This won't be fun."

"Never thought it would be," Pete announced stoically, but a look of fear showed through his bravado.

"So, Pete, how long you been a fisherman? China, would you see if you can find some alcohol that we can use to sterilize this with?" Payton was referring to the hook.

She opened the kit and located a few alcohol pads.

"Aw, about twenty years or so," Pete answered.

The other man returned with the pliers and handed them to Payton.

"China, open one of those and wring the liquid out over the hook and the pliers. It may take two."

She tore the alcohol package and did as he instructed over the hook. As the liquid ran over Pete's finger he winced.

"Now the pliers," Payton said.

China squeezed all she could out of the first pad and then opened another.

"Okay, we're ready to start. China, hold Pete's hand down against the arm of the chair."

She moved around beside Payton and took Pete's wrist securely in her hand.

"I think I'll go see about something in the cabin," the friend stated.

"Yeah, that's just like you, running from a little blood." Pete looked at Payton and nodded his head toward the man. "He faints at the sight of blood."

Payton stopped what he was doing. "Go into the cabin. I don't need to have to stitch you up if you hit your head." Payton waited for the man to disappear into the cabin. "All right, Pete, you may feel a tug when I cut off the eye."

"I'm ready when you are, Doc."

Payton snipped off the end of the hook quickly and surely. Pete let out a yelp.

"Okay, this is going to be the hard part. China, hold him tight. Pete, grip the armrest. Here we go." Putting the flat of the pliers against the top of the hook Payton pushed. China watched as his chew tightened in his effort to not hurt the man and still get the hook to move through the skin.

Pete hissed. Payton leaned into the effort. Time seemed to creep by before the barbed end of the hook made a bump in Pete's skin and then popped through. Pete had turned white.

"Oh, hell," Payton said.

"What's wrong?" China asked, looking at the hook.

"The tip of the hook is missing. It may have broken against the bone or been that way before it went in but either way it's missing."

"What's the problem?" Pete asked in a tight voice.

"It means that I have no choice but to take you to the E.R. It has to be x-rayed."

"I can't pay."

"Let's not worry about that now. You could get an infection and it could kill you if that tip stays in your finger."

"Come on, Doc. Is there no other way?"

"No." Payton said the word as if he was a general giving orders. "China, we'll take him in the car. Let's get the finger covered and get moving."

China pulled out what bandage and tape she could find in the kit and used them to cover the finger, hook and all.

"Hey," Payton called into the cabin to Pete's friend. "We're going to have to take Pete to the E.R."

"What?" the man stuck his head out of the cabin.

"I've got to go to the hospital, man. Come pick me up," Pete said.

"Hold your hand up above you heart and it will help the throbbing," China told Pete, as they walked up the pier. Payton had jogged ahead to get his car and meet them at the entrance of the pier. Payton was pulling up when Pete started to sag beside her. She put an arm around his waist but with his girth she had little chance of holding him upright. The car screeched to a halt and Payton came running to help.

Together they steadied Pete and helped him into the back seat of the car.

"Let's go before he does more damage to himself or one of us." Payton took his seat behind the steering wheel.

With Pete seated and his head lying back against the top of the seat, China said, "I'll ride back here and make sure he doesn't pass out." She climbed into the backseat.

Payton didn't break any laws but he didn't hesitate to move as fast as possible through the traffic. At the hospital, he pulled under the covered emergency entrance. China had her door open and was coming around the car to help with Pete by the time Payton was opening the door. Together, supporting Pete on each side, they walked into the building.

As one of the nurses came toward them Payton announced. "I'm Dr. Jenkins from the walk-in clinic downtown. I need an exam room."

"This way," the nurse said, and directed them to a space.

With Pete's help they were able to get him on the bed and settled.

The E.R. doctor on service that evening entered the room. "What we got here, Payton?"

"Hey, Rick. This is Pete and he had a fish hook in this finger. He needs an x-ray to find the tip."

China was already in the process of removing the bandage as they spoke. When she had it off both men looked at it.

"Well, you're in luck. We aren't busy tonight and therefore neither is X-Ray. Should be able to do one right away. We might want to finish getting that hook out first, though," Rick said.

"Hey, Doc." Pete looked at Payton. "I'd like you to do it."

Payton looked at Rick. He shrugged. "Sure, Pete. If that is what you want."

"I'll get the supplies," China said, and started across the room to the cabinets.

"When's the last time you had a tetanus shot, Pete?"

"Heck, I don't know."

"Then you'll need one before you're released. I'll add it to the chart."

China joined them again and placed what Payton would

need on the stand beside the bed. Payton picked up the needle with the lidocaine in it. "Pete, I'm going to deaden your finger then we'll get this hook out of it."

Pete flinched and moved away. "Hey, I don't like needles."

"You'll like the alternative less. I need you to lay your hand on the bed and look out into the hall. And don't move."

Slowly Payton pushed the thin needle under Pete's skin near the hook. To Pete's credit he didn't cringe and Payton was soon finished. Picking up the pliers China had brought from the supply cabinet, Payton said, "Okay, let's get this done." Payton seized the angry end of the hook with the nose of the pliers and pulled.

As soon as the hook was removed, China placed one of the alcohol pads over the wound.

Pete flinched but didn't jerk away.

Payton dropped the hook in the red biohazardous box. "How are you doing, Pete?"

"Fine." There was a thin white line around Pete's lips.

"Now off to X-Ray. Hopefully we got it all."

"If not, what happens then?"

"I'm afraid surgery." At the puckering of Pete's lips, as if a complaint was forthcoming, Payton said, "Let's not worry about that until we see what an x-ray shows."

The X-ray tech wheeled Pete off.

Twenty minutes later Payton entered the exam room, where China was bandaging Pete's finger. "Well, the radiologist says everything looks great. No foreign objects visible."

Pete's buddy entered the room with a searching look and wide eyes.

"Well, I see your ride is here. When the desk nurse is finished with the paperwork you're free to go."

"Thanks Doc," Pete called, as she and Payton were going

out the door. "You ever want to go fishing, me and my buddy are the ones to come to."

Payton waved a hand above his head in acknowledgment.

"No way I'm I getting on that tub again," he whispered to China.

"Thank goodness. I was afraid you might invite me along."

They laughed. Minutes later, Payton opened the car door for China and she slid into the seat. An air of uncertainty settled over her as he drove through the almost empty parking lot. Would he ask her to come home with him? Did she want to? At the exit Payton paused and looked at her for a long moment before he said, "China, I won't assume but… would you come home with me?"

All that confidence Payton had shown just a few minutes earlier as he'd handled the removal of the hook had gone out the window. He was as insecure about their relationship as she was. Somehow that reassured her.

She nodded. A huge smile covered his face as he took her hand and placed it on his thigh before he pulled out into the traffic.

Somewhere after midnight Payton rolled over and kissed her shoulder before his mouth found hers. His hand cupped a breast, teasing the nipple. This time their lovemaking was slow and easy. Later, much later, China curled up next to his warm body and inhaled deeply. Her eyes slowly closed on an exhalation.

Life could be safe and secure.

"So, do you want to go parasailing with me today?" Payton asked, as he placed kisses across her belly midmorning of the next day.

"What?"

"You know, where someone pulls you behind the boat and you're attached to a parachute and you go up in the air."

She rolled her eyes and said in a sarcastic voice, "I know what parasailing is. I just wanted to know why you would want to do it."

"Because I never have."

"Do you have a death wish or something?"

Payton tensed.

"I'm sorry. I didn't think. It hard for me to imagine you having had cancer. You seem so hearty."

"I am hearty."

"You know what I mean."

Payton sat up and looked at the majestically beautiful woman before him who had no idea how much she affected his world. "I know. I just like giving you a hard time."

"Will you tell me about it?" she asked softly.

Payton hesitated. Did she really want to know all the gory details? She deserved to. With a resigned release of a breath he said, "I worked long hours in the E.R. in the largest trauma center in Chicago. I didn't mind. I loved what I did. Everything gave me an adrenaline rush. I'm from a long line of doctors. In fact, my great-grandfather was on the board when the hospital opened. My father sits on the board today."

"You were headed that way too," China said, as a statement of fact.

"Yeah. I was on the fast track with the in-crowd ticket. But I got sick. I didn't see it coming or maybe I didn't want to admit it. I started feeling tired. Then I found the lump in my neck."

He couldn't miss the soft intake of China's breath. To her credit, she didn't say anything.

"I couldn't ignore any longer that something was seriously wrong. If I had been one of my patients I would've chewed me out for not going to the doctor sooner. I went to see my best buddy and…" Payton grinned "…he did chew me out. There was a biopsy, the bad news radiation and chemo. My parents came unglued. My fiancée handed my ring back."

"Not much of a person, in my opinion." She sounded like a warrior fighting for her family. He liked the sound of it.

"Thank you. I agree. It hurt at the time but in hindsight I don't think we would've made it anyway. She was far more interested in my family name and its influence than me."

China smiled at him. "Well, I'm glad she let you go, otherwise I might not have met you."

He gave her an appreciative kiss. "Thank you. I feel the same way about you."

"So how did your family react to your diagnosis?"

"The same way they do to everything. He'll overcome this.' My mom became my major caregiver. I'll forever be grateful to her."

"I hear a but in there."

"Well, Mom almost became oppressive with her help. She was worried about losing me and I understand that, but when I began to get better she had a hard time accepting I needed her to back off."

"I'm guessing she didn't take it well when you decided to move down here."

"No, and neither did my father. They wanted me close because they love me and are concerned about me but they were also upset that I would give up all they considered important, like my position at the hospital, my influence in the community, to move down here to nothing." When China stiffened he was quick to say. "Sorry, those are their words, not mine. To say they didn't understand I had changed or I needed to move my life in a different direction would be an understatement."

"I know that this isn't any of my business but are you

seeing someone regularly for check-ups?" The note of concern in her voice didn't escape his notice.

"Yes, Nurse China. I'm taking care of myself. I have regular bloodwork done. I'm going to Chicago next month for a checkup." His look met hers. "Hey, why don't you go with me?"

China was surprised to find at she rather liked the idea of meeting Payton's family. "How about we see when the time comes?" If she made that step, she would be trusting that there was something more between them than just being bed friends.

"Okay, I'll let it go for now but what about that parasailing?"

"How about I watch you?"

"It would be a lot more fun if you went up with me. We could make out, maybe try a little something else."

China laughed and swatted him playfully. "You're trying to live dangerously again."

Payton ran a hand from her foot up along her calf and smiled when she shivered. "Yes, maybe I am, but it sounds like fun, doesn't it?" He dropped his voice to a sexy persuasive tone.

She smiled. "I could just kiss you before you go up."

"That's not the same. Come on, China. I think it would be fun." He gave her a pleading look.

"Okay, if I agree to do that, what are you going to do for me?"

China felt her cheeks growing warm in reaction to Payton's wolfish grin. She swallowed the lump of anticipation in her throat. "That would be nice but I really had something else in mind."

He narrowed his eyes. "Like what?"

"Like going to a botanical garden."

His look became unsure, as if spending the day looking

at plants wasn't his idea of fun. To his credit he said, "Sure. How about Tuesday? We're both off."

"How do you know that?"

"I checked the schedule."

"Are you stalking me?" She gave him a dubious look.

Payton moved in close, becoming predatory. "And if I were?"

China liked it that he'd been interested enough to check on when she worked. With hooded eyes she said, "I guess I don't mind."

"Since I can't talk you into going parasailing with me today, how about we spend the day on the beach? Maybe try some skinny-dipping?"

"That sounds like fun but I make no promises about the skinny-dipping."

"Given time, I bet I can convince you it would be fun." He grabbed her and tugged her to him, suppressing her giggle when his lips found hers.

CHAPTER NINE

PAYTON HAD TO admit the day had been more interesting than he'd anticipated. China had almost hummed with her excitement over visiting the Beaumont Botanical Gardens. Her reaction mimicked his to the thoughts of going sailing or, better yet, having China beneath him. He could appreciate that delight.

He'd picked her up early Tuesday morning. They'd stopped by Dolly's for donuts and coffee on their way out of town. "So, do you have directions?"

"I do. It's only about four hours away."

"Four hours!"

"Did I forget to tell you that?" she said in a sugar-sweet voice.

He chuckled. "I think I've been had. I'm glad we don't have to be at work until two tomorrow. We're going to make a day of it and a night." At least he'd have China to himself for a good long time.

"I didn't bring anything to stay overnight."

He wiggled his brows. "You won't need it."

"Now I think I'm the one being had."

"Oh, I plan to."

China turned pink before she leaned back and gazed out his sunroof. "Looks like we're going to have a nice day. The last time I went to a botanical garden it rained. It was still wonderful but I didn't enjoy riding home damp."

"You walked around in the rain to see a garden?" Disbelief filled his voice.

"Sure, why not? It's a different world when it rains."

She did truly love this stuff. He was learning a different facet of China. Would he ever learn them all?

Payton enjoyed the drive. His family had always flown when taking vacations. Making long road trips had never really been his thing but he'd taken pleasure in the freedom he'd had when driving down from Chicago. He given credit to his smooth-driving car for making that trip fun but spending time with China on this one was far better. It was also fascinating to see the miles and miles of swamp as they motored through Louisiana. He'd seen pictures of the land but nothing compared to the view from bridge after long bridge over untamed acreage.

He and China chatted about nothing in particular, argued over what was the best fast-food restaurant, both agreeing that a chicken sandwich was far better than a hamburger. They even sang along at the top of their lungs with the radio, like two college students escaping on spring break.

The more time he spent with China the more he discovered he enjoyed being around her. That was in bed as well as out. All in all it was a pleasant morning and far more entertaining than he would have imagined.

But could it continue? Should he let it? Would she leave him if he got sick? No, but China had such a caring heart that she could become like his mom about his illness. He didn't want that. It would kill their relationship just as surely as if she walked out on him. Right now he was going to make the most of their time together.

Just before lunch he drove into the paved parking lot of the botanical gardens.

They were on their way to the entrance when China

asked, "Are you hungry? If you are, we can get something at the vending machines."

He took her hand. "I'm open to whatever you want to do. This is your day."

She smiled up at him with such happiness in her eyes that it hit him like a fist to the chest. He'd like to always be the one to put that look on her face. Heaven help him, was there ever a better feeling? He returned her smile.

"Okay, then. I want to look. Those donuts I had are still with me." China took his hand. It was the first time she'd ever initiated a contact in public. He liked knowing she felt he was hers to touch.

"Maybe you should have thought a little longer about having that third donut."

She stopped and glared at him. "What're you trying to say? I'm getting fat?"

Payton put a hand over his heart. "No way." He slowly looked at her from the top of her head to her feet. She looked breathtaking in her light blue dress that showed her legs off. "No, I'd say you're just about perfect."

She giggled. A sound he treasured.

"Thanks. I do love it when you pour on the charm."

They started walking again. He lowered his chin, giving her a disbelieving look. "I put on charm?"

"Sure you do. You play Jean like a fine violin."

Payton brow wrinkled. "What does that mean?"

"That you sweet-talk her into getting your way." She glanced at him. There was a twinkle in her eyes.

"I do not."

China stopped and put her hands on her hips. "You didn't think she wouldn't mention that you'd talked her into changing your schedule?"

He had the good grace to look contrite. "Well..." He drew the word out. "I might have done that. But in my defense, I wanted to spend the day with you."

China squeezed his hand and grinned.

Oh, yeah, he had it bad.

"Thanks. I think that's the nicest thing anyone has ever done for me."

They'd reached the information stand.

"There's no charge?" In his Chicago world he was charged for everything.

"Nope. Plants lovers, you know." China pulled a map of the gardens out of a rack.

Payton looked over her shoulder. "So, have you decided what we're going to do?"

"I have. We're going to take this path through the formal gardens, then down to the water gardens, and around this way." She used her finger to show him the path.

"Maybe I should have said stop by the vending machine after all. That looks like I might need to fortify myself for the trip."

"Come on. If you pass out I promise to leave you and come back for you later," she said in a kidding tone.

He chuckled. "You're a hard woman, Ms. Davis."

"No, I just don't want to miss a minute of the gardens. I've been trying to come here for years."

"Why haven't you?"

"I guess time, and my parents needed me." She shrugged. "I didn't have someone to enjoy the gardens with."

He looped her arm through the crook of his. "It's not parasailing but I'm glad I came."

They'd started down a path between knee-high box-woods when China said, "I'm glad you did too."

Some time later they entered a wooded area. "These are pretty. What type of plant is this?" Payton asked.

"Southern azalea. There're thousands of varieties. They come in all colors—pink, red, white. Many more."

"My mom would love these. She'd have the gardener planting some at her house if she only knew."

"It would be a waste of the gardener's time. They don't grow well that far north."

She reached out and touched a petal of a flower gently.

It suddenly struck him that China would make a wonderful mom. "Okay, lesson learned."

"Well, that's a first. I taught the smartest doctor I know something."

Payton squared his shoulders and puffed out his chest as if he were a peacock, strutting. "I'm the smartest doctor you know?"

"Don't let it go to your head, Doc. But you are the best I've seen. You were great with Pete."

He leaned in close, as if he was going to tell her a secret. "You're not just saying that because you like other things about me?"

She pushed him away. "Please." She grinned. "You do think highly of yourself."

"Those little noises of pleasure you make at just the right moment might make me believe you think I'm pretty nice." She did have a way of making him feeling special. Something no other woman had ever done. Because of her admiration his male ego was in fine form.

A blush covered her cheeks and she looked away. "Quit trying to embarrass me and let's go and see the water garden. The pictures of it remind me of Monet's water lilies paintings."

"Now, those I know. Mom has one hanging in the living room."

"Figures," China muttered, as she led the way.

By midafternoon they'd found a small café that offered sandwiches and a shady place to eat. China took a seat at a small rod iron table for two under a huge oak that was part of the patio area belonging to the café. She watched as Payton joined her with a heart filled with happiness.

Payton's hair had grown over the weeks. There was a slight wave to it now. It felt warm and soft in her fingers. That she knew well from the number of times she'd run her fingers through it. He wore dark glasses against the sun but behind them were eyes of pure blue that twinkled when he teased, and he did that often. Her family wasn't that type. It was seductive to have someone notice her enough that they teased her. Payton had a way of making her feel important, not just being around because she was needed to help.

He put down the tray with the food and sat. They ate quietly, each lost in their own thoughts. Payton was really a fine-looking man, nice, caring, divine lover…

"You're staring at me. I really don't mind beautiful women doing that—"

"Sorry."

"What were you thinking?"

"That I should say thank you for bringing me today."

Payton took her hand and squeezed it then let it go. "It has been my pleasure and I mean that. You might have something with the 'stop and smell the roses' idea."

She grinned at him. "I hope that wasn't just a pun."

"No pun, just a thought."

"So you found out that you can feel alive without an adrenaline rush." She picked up her sandwich.

He met her gaze. "Was today about proving a point?"

She shook her head. "No, but it didn't hurt if I did. I don't think life is about what we do but about who and what we love."

"I love to sail."

"Yes. But why? What is there about sailing you love?"

Payton looked off into space a moment before returning his gaze to hers. "I love the way the water laps against the hull when I'm lying on my back, looking up at a blue sky."

"That—" her voice had a snap of awe in it "—is what living really is."

"Okay, Miss Know-it-All. What's really living for you?"

She almost blurted out, "Being with you," but she caught the words before they passed her lips. "When I put my hands down in rich soil and feel it crumble between my fingers. Or smell the wholesome goodness of where the sun kissed it."

"You didn't even have to think about your answer."

She met his gaze. "No, I didn't. I recognized that a long time ago. It's where I feel like I belong. Where I feel happy and secure."

"Security is important to you?"

"Yeah, I guess it is. I never really had it after Chad left. I was always afraid I'd mess up and Father would be telling me to get out. So, what are you looking for?"

He took a long moment to think. "I really don't know."

"You want to know what I think?"

"I don't know. Do I?"

She smirked. "I think you're looking for contentment."

"You're starting to sound like one of those Eastern gurus."

China picked up her drink cup. "I'm no guru. I just know that you can't always be chasing something to feel alive. The simple, slow-down method works for me. I think you need to look at why you need adventure or danger to feel alive."

"You might be getting a little preachy now."

She wrinkled her nose. "Sorry. That wasn't what I meant to do. How you spend your time really isn't my business anyway."

He captured her hand again and her gaze. "I'd like to be your business."

China's heart thumped faster.

"I think we have something special here, China. I'd like to believe that I'm your business and you're mine."

She gifted him with an easy smile of acceptance. "I'd like that too."

Payton leaned in and gave her a gentle kiss that assured her he meant every word.

Three hours later, he pulled the car to a stop in front of a magical, historical hotel in the French Quarter of New Orleans, complete with filigree rod iron balconies, huge green shutters and a wooden, cut-glass door. A young man dressed in red livery circled the car to stand at Payton's door.

"Payton, this is too much," China said in a voice breathy with amazement.

"Why?"

"I would've been comfortable with a roadside hotel."

"You would have but I wouldn't. I've stayed here a number of times. They had a room open, we needed one, so here we are."

"Figures." Payton moved in a more affluent world than hers. There was his need for adventure also. She wasn't always comfortable with either of those. Kelsey would appreciate his need for fast living. *Kelsey.* China missed her. Wished she could share some sister time and tell Kelsey about Payton and the way he made her feel.

Payton had stepped out of the car and leaned down to look at her. "How's that?"

"You get what you want."

"Sweetheart, all I want right now is a hot bath and you, and not necessarily in that order."

She didn't miss his satisfied grin of male pride before he flipped the valet the keys and came round to help her out of the car. He offered her his arm and they walked into the lobby.

"It's unreal." China looked past the polished oak registration desk to the open courtyard beyond with a bubbling fountain.

He smiled indulgently and said, as if he were speaking to a child, "Go on out and look at the plants. I know you want to. Our room is across the courtyard so I'll meet you out there."

China gingerly touched the palm that towered over her head and studied the ground cover, which had been carefully cared for, until Payton joined her. He took her hand without comment, led her up the outdoor staircase and along the open walkway above the courtyard until they reached a door located furthest from the busy street outside the hotel.

Payton placed an old-fashioned skeleton style key into the lock and swung the door open. Taking one long step into the room, he tugged her in after him and pushed the door closed.

"Wha—?"

"This is what!" His mouth took hers as his hands lifted and brought her up against his sturdy body. The evidence of his desire stood thick between them. China wrapped her arms around his neck. Payton's hands cupped her behind. He backed to the bed, bringing her down on top of him as he lay on the mattress of the canopied oak four-poster bed.

Her lips left his. She tilted back, still straddling his hips. "Beautiful bed."

Payton growled, "Forget the decor. I'm going to show you how comfortable it is." He rolled her over and took her lips again.

Once again his life had been turned upside down. Payton smiled. At least this time he was enjoying it. To have China wake in his arms was the height of satisfaction. They had spent the entire night in New Orleans in bed making love and sharing room service. He owed her another visit so they could get out and be tourists for a while. They'd returned to Golden Shores in enough time to change and get to work on time.

Payton was grateful they were busy. Every time he met China's gaze her eyes held this dreamy look that remind him of the time they'd spent together and he wanted her all over again. She'd give him a Cheshire cat grin as she passed him in the hall and he'd be hard for her.

Did she feel the same way? What if he got sick again? The questions went on and on. What he did know was that he was going to enjoy every minute he could with her.

They both, thankfully and disappointingly, had opposite shifts the rest of the week. They shared the weekend off and spent the time sailing, swimming, tending plants and, best of all, making love. He should have guessed by China's spirited attitude that she might be rather aggressive in the bedroom but when she'd become the aggressor during their lovemaking he'd almost embarrassed himself by losing control.

On the Monday afternoon after their amazing weekend Payton flipped a chart closed and stared out into space. He had sworn that after Janice he'd never let himself truly open up to a woman again. He'd started over in a new place with a new chance at life, a dream home and a place to live life to the fullest. Then what happened? China.

He glanced at his watch. One-thirty. China would be in at two. To his great woe he and China were working opposite shifts again all week. She'd insisted that he take her home the night before. It had almost killed him but he'd done as she'd requested. Her reasoning had been that she needed her sleep and he wasn't letting her have any.

It had been so long for him and he found China irresistible. She hadn't complained and she was always eager to please. Maybe he'd demanded too much. She'd seemed reluctant to leave him during their long kiss that had had him hot for her again before she'd climbed the stairs to her apartment. In fact, if he hadn't been afraid he'd sound pathetic, he would've beg to go up with her.

Heaven help him, he had it bad. If he didn't pull it together he'd pounce on China the second she entered the clinic. Robin, Jean and Doris would appreciate that show but he had no doubt that China wouldn't. He glanced at his watch again. With a snort of disgust he pulled another chart off the stack.

Payton sensed China before he looked up to find her standing in the doorway.

"Hey," she said almost shyly.

"Hey." He grinned and came around the desk. To his disappointment, Larry came up behind her.

China didn't know what she was thinking when she stopped by Payton's office. That wasn't her habit when she came in for her shift but she'd been dying to see him. Even her gardening hadn't interfered with her daydreaming about him. She'd relived every moment they'd spent together, had even started to believe they might be building something lasting. Still, the closer she'd come to work time the more insecure she'd become. Maybe he'd just wanted her because she'd been available. He'd been sick, she was the first girl...

With nervous jitters, she'd approached his door and spoken. She had been relieved to see Payton smile and heat had come to his eyes. The same disappointment she felt showed on his face when Larry stepped up behind her. Just a look as simple and unsolicited as his made her stomach flutter. A warm, mushy feeling washed over her.

For all her believing she'd never let it happen, she'd fallen hopelessly in love with Payton.

"Hi, China," Larry said, as he squeezed by her into the

office. "I'm not interrupting anything, am I?" He glanced at Payton and then at her.

"No," she and Payton said in unison.

Larry gave them both curious looks. She lowered her eyes and said, "I'll let you two talk."

China took a report from Robin then headed down the hall to speak to the two patients who were waiting in the exam rooms. Payton met her coming up the hall. He glanced around then grabbed her arm and pulled her into an empty exam room. Closing the door, he leaned back against it and brought her against him.

"I'm not leaving without this." His lips found hers.

Any concern she'd had that Payton might not still be interested in her vanished. His mouth was hot and heavy, asking, begging and taking. She tugged his knit collared shirt from his pants and slipped her hands underneath, finding his warm skin, letting her fingers trail around to his back.

One long delicious kiss later China pulled away. Payton's eyes held an intensity that said he wanted more. He desire pressed thickly against her. She sighed. Nothing had changed.

She said softly, "Payton, this isn't the time or place."

He let his forehead rest against hers. "I know. Can I see you tonight after you get off?"

"My parents are expecting me for dinner tonight."

He let her step away but didn't release her. "I'd love to meet your parents."

Was she ready for that? That wasn't a step forward she was sure she could make. What would Payton think of them?

"I don't know."

"Why? I've got to meet them some time. Come on, China. You're not ashamed of me, are you?" He grinned.

How could she say no? The man she loved should know everything about her. Especially her parents. "Don't be silly. If you want to go then be here at seven."

* * *

Payton was sitting in the parking lot talking on the phone with his friend and physician when China slipped into the passenger seat. He smiled in welcome.

"Yes, John. I'll have it redrawn tomorrow first thing."

"This won't wait, Payton. None of that pretending it will go away stuff. There may be nothing to it but I'm not taking any chances at this stage."

"I understand. I'll be a model patient, I promise."

"That'll be a change for the better."

"Funny, buddy, very funny."

"Tomorrow. No excuses."

"I got the message. Later, John."

Concern marred China's features. "What was that all about?"

"Nothing. Just a friendly reminder to have my blood drawn."

"That's all there is to it, isn't there?"

"Yes." He leaned over and gave her a quick kiss on the lips before starting the car.

She gave him a suspicious look. "You would tell me if something is wrong?"

"China, stop fussing. I'm fine. Leave it alone," he said, more sharply than he'd intended.

"I only asked because—"

He took her hand and squeezed it. "I know you care. Okay, which way to your parents'?"

"They live out the Bay Road but we've got to stop by the grocery store first."

He backed the car out of the parking spot. "What? You don't do the grocery shopping?"

"Mom needs a few things and she asked me to stop by and get them."

"Is she sick?"

"No. Why?"

"I was just wondering why she couldn't do her own shopping." Payton pulled into the main street and headed toward the store.

"She mentioned she needed to pick up a few things and I offered to get them for her. Do you have a problem stopping?"

"No, I was just surprised, that's all."

Forty-five minutes later Payton turned the car into the crushed shell drive China indicated. It was a simple board and batten house on stilts, facing the bay. Painted a light gray and trimmed in white, it was similar to the other homes lining the road. It had a long green manicured lawn that met a pier that stretched out into the water. Plants graced the porch that wrapped around the place on three sides. It was obviously a well cared-for home.

Payton gathered the grocery bags from the trunk and followed China up the steps to wait beside her at the front door. A woman with short gray hair and world-weariness about her mouth greeted them at the door. She offered a smile that didn't reach her eyes. How long had it been since she'd been truly happy?

"Hi, honey, come on in." Mrs. Davis stepped back and allowed China and Payton to enter.

"Mama, this is Payton Jenkins."

"Welcome, Payton. China told me she was bringing a friend. It's nice to meet you."

At one time being China's friend had sounded good but now he wanted to be more. "Hi, Mrs. Davis. It's nice to meet you."

She closed the door and led them into a large, comfortable-looking room.

"China, I've waited for you to start dinner."

Payton looked at China. She seemed okay with the arrangement. Why wasn't her mom cooking? China had been at work all afternoon.

"Well, I'll get started on the potatoes. I guess Father will want pork chops. I'll add a salad as well. Father should be home soon, shouldn't he?"

"Yes, I expect him any minute."

"Payton, you can bring those in here." China indicated the bags he still held. He followed her through the living room into the kitchen. It was much smaller than his but efficient-looking. He placed the groceries on the counter.

"Why don't you go out and talk to Mom while I get supper together?" China reached for a bag and started to unpack it.

Leaning his hip against the counter, he said, "You don't want my help?"

"No, I'll get it."

What was going on? China hated to go grocery shopping and wasn't that big a fan of cooking. He reluctantly left her and returned to the living room.

"Payton, come in and make yourself at home. China can handle dinner. Have a seat." Mrs. Davis indicated a chair across the room from the one she was taking.

Payton sank into the overstuffed chair. Further across the room sat a well-used recliner. It had to belong to China's father. On a table near by Payton saw a grouping of pictures of a boy at various stages in his life. The arrangement reminded him of a shrine. The pictures had to be of China's brother. His disappearance hung like a shroud over the family. Payton scanned the room and only found one picture of China and another of a girl that could only be her sister.

"So, Payton, are you from around here?" Mrs. Davis asked.

"No, I'm from Chicago."

She gave him a look of interest. "Chicago? Well, you're a long way from home."

"I am."

"Are you here on vacation?"

Before Payton could answer the question, what had to be the door from the carport area below opened and an average-sized man with thinning hair entered. He wasn't the big burly man Payton had pictured from China's description of him.

"Hi, Father," China chirped, in an overly happy voice.

"Hi. What's for supper?"

"Pork chops, of course. They're your favorite, aren't they?" She stepped out of the kitchen and kissed him on the cheek. "Father, I'd like you to meet Payton Jenkins. He works with me."

The man turned his piercing look to Payton as if interrogating him. For a second Payton almost squirmed under Mr. Davis's scrutiny but caught himself. He returned a level gaze. Hadn't China said her father was a rigid man? Payton was too old, had been through too much to let someone intimidate him. He rose and offered his outstretched hand to Mr. Davis, who took it in a sound handshake that made Payton believe he might have gained some respect.

"Father, supper should be ready in about fifteen minutes."

"Good, I'm hungry."

"Hi, hon," Mr. Davis said, stepping over to kiss Mrs. Davis on the forehead.

"I think I'll see if I can help China." Payton stood and headed for the kitchen. Was he imagining that the atmosphere had turned cooler and the women tensed when the head of the house had come in? The click-click of the recliner footrest cranking up told Payton that Mr. Davis had taken his chair.

Some time later, Payton helped China place the platters of food on the table.

"Supper," she called.

Payton saw Mrs. Davis rise from her chair. "Please, come

join us, Jim," she said, low enough that Payton had the impression that she didn't want him to hear her pleading.

"No, I'll just eat here. I've had a long day."

Payton's mom might not have been the one to cook the meal but she'd seen to it that their family had always shared the evening meal together. That was one point his mom had never wavered on. Payton's father would have never gotten away with China's father's attitude.

"Mama, I'll fix him a plate. Come on and join us." China picked up one of the plates off the table.

Payton watched, amazed, as she hurriedly spooned food in large portions onto it. China also worked all day and now she was playing server girl to her father? What had happened to the person who had stood up to him so many times?

China had just finished putting food on her own plate when her father called from the other room, "This pork chop is a little too done."

"I'm sorry, Father. You can have mine." China jumped up and headed to the living area with her plate in her hand.

Payton shook his head in disbelief. It took all his self-control not to take the plate from her and drag her out of the house. China had turned into a super-pleaser. Couldn't she see that her father was manipulating her? Had she been doing this for years?

When his look caught her mom's she smiled. Didn't she see what was going on? She acted as if China's actions were natural. They certainly appeared to be the norm in this house. He saw them as very dysfunctional and unhealthy.

China brought back her father's half of a pork chop on her plate. Going into the kitchen, she returned with no meat on her plate. She took her seat but didn't meet his gaze. He cut what was left of his meat and placed it on her plate. She glanced at him in surprise, as if everyone, including her, expected her to go without part of her meal.

"So, Payton, you were telling me what brought you to Golden Shores," Mrs. Davis said in an almost apologetic tone.

They carried on a conversation with no further interaction with China's father. After dinner, Payton helped China do the dishes. When they left she kissed her father on the forehead. He acknowledged her with a grunt and continued to watch his TV show. Payton wanted to shake the man. Didn't he realize what a wonderful person China was? She deserved to be treated better by her family. Payton said good evening to the man, whose only response was to raise a hand briefly.

At his car, Payton opened the door for China then got in himself. He turned to her. "Exactly what happen in there?"

She gave him a puzzled look. "What do you mean?"

"The way you acted."

"How's that?"

"Like a servant. As if you couldn't speak up for yourself."

"They're my parents. I didn't do anything that I haven't always done. They need me."

What if he got sick again? Would she treat him the same way she had her father? Care for him more out of guilt than love? He wanted to be loved for who he was, not because someone needed to be needed. He couldn't, wouldn't put himself or China through that. They both deserved more. Janice may have hurt him but at least she'd been honest about what she could take. Could China bring herself to do that if he became ill again? Could he afford to take the chance of finding out?

"China, you actually gave your father your meal." He didn't try to keep his disbelief out of his voice. "Even more astounding is that he took it without argument."

"He's my father," she said in an ashamed voice.

"But that doesn't mean you should let him walk all

over you. As strong a person as I've seen you be, not only with me but in medical situations, and you become a completely different person when you're around your parents. Why?"

"I don't."

"Yes, you do."

"They're all I have."

"No, they're not. You've got a sister."

"She doesn't have anything to do with us."

"After what I just saw, I'm not surprised."

"You're going too far now."

"I don't think so. I care about you and I know how you act around your parents isn't healthy. What're you afraid of? That if you're not the perfect child that your father will give you the same ultimatum he gave your brother and your mom will let it happen? You're an adult now. You don't have to have their blessing anymore. Don't you think it's time for you to have a life not controlled by them? When was the last time you told them you wouldn't be cooking supper when you came over? Do they even know that you hate the grocery store?"

"That's enough, Payton."

"China, you can't make up for the fact that they don't know where your brother is or ease their guilt. They have to learn to live with the past just like you do. You have to find security without living in fear of their rejection. What I saw tonight was you trying to keep the peace at all costs. That's not good for you or them."

"They've already lost two children. If I don't come around—"

"Then maybe they'll have to deal with each other and the way things are. They can handle life without you holding their hands."

She turned to him, her jaw clenched and lips drawn into a tight, thin line. "Well, it must be nice to sit on the outside and look in. To know what everyone else should do Mr. I-ran-away-from-home-because-I-couldn't-take-the-pressure."

"I didn't run away from home. I decided to live elsewhere. Take my life in a different direction."

"Some of us don't have that luxury. Like my brother… When life got too hard in one place, you just picked up and left. Sometimes you have to stay and deal with what is happening. I learned to deal the best way I know how. You haven't even made an effort to really talk to your parents, have you? Explain how you really feel? I don't see that we're all that different. What I know is that you can point out others' issues but you can't see your own."

That stung. More than he wanted to admit. "My parents have expectations, demands."

"And you don't think mine do?" she threw back at him.

"I know yours do but you don't need to let them make you feel like you're twelve again when all you want to do is please them so you can feel loved."

"I'm sorry I'm not who you think I should be." She opened the door. "I'll get Mom to drive me home. Thanks for a wonderful evening," she spat, and slammed the door.

Payton watched in disbelief as China stalked off. Had he just been hit by a Gulf storm? What had just happened? How could she not see what her parents were doing to her?

Surely when she calmed down China would come around. In the scheme of things, what they were fighting over was nothing. He knew life and death and this wasn't it. He'd give her some room to cool down and then they'd work it out. What they had together was too good to let go of just like that.

He slowly backed out of the drive. With one last glance back at the house he drove down the road, leaving an even bigger gap between them.

* * *

China couldn't remember a more uncomfortable discussion with her mom than trying to explain why she'd stomped back into the house and asked for a ride home. She'd didn't want to talk about Payton. He was wrong. She didn't do what he accused her of doing.

She spent a horrible evening, crying, and compounded it with tossing and turning before emotional exhaustion took her. Who did Payton think he was talking to? How had something so wonderful turned so ugly with only a few words? Payton had real nerve. Had she misjudged him just as she had another man she'd cared about? She'd been right about him in the first place.

As if the fates were ganging up against her, one of Larry's children had a school field trip and Larry had asked Payton to switch shifts with him. China managed to make it through the shift without interacting with Payton except when it had to do with a patient. He didn't seem any more eager to speak to her then she was to him.

China looked at her wristwatch. Only thirty more minutes. Her nerves were strung out tighter than a banjo string. She'd even snapped at Doris, which had got her a look of surprise. Thankfully a patient had come in and prevented Doris from asking questions.

At one minute to two China had her purse under her arm and was on the way toward the back door. She needed to plan something. Clear her mind. Figure out how to deal with Payton. How to fix things between them or at least learn to work with him without the burning hurt boiling over. Maybe she needed to see about transferring to the hospital.

"Yes, I understand." Payton's voice drifted out into the hall as she passed the office door.

She'd planned to keep on walking, not glance in his direction, but couldn't help herself. His shoulders were slumped and his elbows were propped on the desk with his dark-haired head in his hands. Something was wrong. Was he sick? Had he gotten bad news? She couldn't leave without knowing. They might be through but that didn't stop her from caring.

With her heart racing she asked from the doorway, "Payton, what's wrong?"

He raised his head. "Nothing."

The shadowed look in his eyes told her differently. She stepped further into the room. "What's going on? Are you feeling okay?"

"I'm fine."

"It doesn't look that way."

He stood. "I'm fine, really. I'm sorry if I hurt your feelings yesterday. I'm sorry if I'm hurting them now. But I think we have run our course."

She jerked back as if he'd slapped her. She'd expected this. He wasn't saying anything she didn't already know but she didn't like hearing it verbalized, especially in such a cold voice. She known it was over the second she'd seen that look of disbelief on his face. Not wanting to admit it, last night she'd had no choice but to face the facts. That didn't mean it didn't feel like her heart was breaking into a thousand pieces and being flung to the ends of the earth.

Refusing to run and hide, she choked out the words, "I agree."

For a second had there been hurt in his eyes?

"To make things easier, I'll see about transferring to another clinic or to the E.R."

Unable to say more, she nodded. Her greatest fear had come true. She didn't measure up. He'd said he didn't want her.

"I'm sorry."

China nodded again. With a force of will she hadn't known she had, she made her feet move. In a daze of pain, anger and disappointment and holding back the tears that threatened, she stumbled out the back door.

Payton closed the door to the office and sank into the desk chair. His head dropped into his hands. He'd been sick after chemo but he'd never felt as nauseated as he had when he'd seen the look on China's face. He'd known what he'd had to do, but that hadn't made it any easier. His bloodwork had come back abnormal. He couldn't, wouldn't take her on that ride with him if cancer had returned. China deserved a better life. A more secure one. She would spend her days caring for him, and he couldn't have that. He wouldn't let her sit by his bed and worry. His parents would be bad enough.

China would move on from him soon enough, he decided, but he wouldn't be so lucky. She wasn't someone he'd ever get over.

CHAPTER TEN

CHINA COULDN'T REMEMBER feeling more miserable than she had been in the last week. The only upside was that she didn't have to hold it together in front of Payton. He hadn't been at the clinic and she'd refused to ask why. She'd just figured that he'd managed to get a quick transfer or had taken a few days off.

She looked awful. No matter what she did—cold water to the eyes, drops, even cucumber slices—she still couldn't get the puffiness to recede from crying herself to sleep. She missed Payton's arms around her, his hard body against her back, his wit, his smile.

Doris and Jean had given her puzzled looks but hadn't asked questions. Robin wasn't as tactful. She cornered China in the supply room.

"So, what gives with Payton? You know where he is?"

China opened a cabinet and pulled out gloves, tissues and tongue depressors to replace those used in the exam rooms. "No. I haven't spoken to him."

"I thought you two were tight."

"Tight?"

Robin gave a disgusted snort. "Don't play dumb with me. We all know you and Payton were having a thing. You could see it any time you two were together."

China suppressed a groan. Had they been that obvious?

She closed the cabinet. "Well, if we did have a 'thing,' we don't anymore. I've not spoken to him in days."

"Jean did let it slip that he'd gone to Chicago. You think he's moving back there?"

China gathered the supplies in her arms. "You know, Robin, I really have no idea," she said, as she left the room.

Entering an exam room, she pushed the door closed with her elbow. She dumped the supplies in a heap on the table, sank into the chair and put her head into her hands before all the pain she felt flowed out. Some time later, she wiped the moisture away with the back of her hand and straightened her shoulders. It was time she pulled herself together. Got her life back to normal. Learned to live without Payton. She done it before he'd come to town and she'd do it again. Her parents were expecting her to cook dinner tonight, she'd focus on that.

China finished cleaning off the table and straightening her parents' kitchen. Her father was in his chair with the news on the TV but the volume down as he read the paper. Her mom focused on one of her many craft projects. There was no interaction between them or even China. They hadn't even asked about Payton. It was as if they were going through the motions of life but never really living it. She wanted more than that. Had lived it with Payton.

When had her family dynamics become so twisted? Was that why Kelsey never visited? Maybe it was time to ask her? See if she could reestablish some kind of solid relationship with at least one member of her family.

It had taken some persuading on China's part to get Kelsey to agree to meet. She'd not out and out said no. Instead, Kelsey seemed to have an excuse for being busy on every date China suggested. When China finally said, "This isn't about Mom and Dad. This is about me. Things I need to know," Kelsey agreed.

China watched Kelsey pull into the parking spot from the front window of the tearoom on Main Street.

Where China had dark hair cut conservatively, Kelsey was fair-haired with a trendy cut that stuck up on her head. China was petite and Kelsey was tall with an athlete's body. They couldn't be more different yet they had shared the same upbringing.

China stood as the bell on the door tinkled, announcing Kelsey's entrance. Opening her arms in welcome, China saw Kelsey's second of hesitation before she stepped into her embrace. They released each other. China smiled. "Thank you for coming. I've missed you."

Kelsey gave her a weary smile as they sat down in the antique wooden chairs at their table. China ran her hands across the tablecloth, as if smoothing out a wrinkle that didn't exist.

A middle-aged woman wearing a white ruffled apron came to take their order. After she left Kelsey said, "Please don't try to convince me I need to see Mom and Father."

"Like I said on the phone, I won't do that, but I would like to ask you some questions about them."

"China, I don't want to talk about them."

"The questions have to do with me. You're the only person I know to ask. I need to know."

Kelsey's brow wrinkled and she twisted her mouth upward. "What's going on?"

"I need to know…"

Kelsey put her elbow on the table and leaned toward China.

"Uh, a friend of mine said I act differently when I'm around Mom and Dad. Do you think that's true?"

"Hell, yes, you do!"

China jerked at the force of Kelsey's reply.

"I hated the way they treated you but I think I hated it more that you let them treat you that way."

"I didn't see it," China said softly, "until Payton pointed it out."

"Payton?"

"A friend."

The woman returned to serve them their tea then left silently.

Kelsey nodded. "Something happened to you after Chad left. You couldn't do enough to make Mom and Father happy, especially Father. You never stood up to them, no matter how unreasonable they were. You were always trying to make things better, smooth things over."

"Why haven't you said something before?"

"I was young, but I knew when you were trying to hide what I was doing from Mom and Father. You covered for me, and even lied for me on occasion, but I hated what I saw them doing to you."

Had her fear of stepping out of line and being rejected been that strong? "I didn't know they were doing anything to me. I just didn't want them to get mad at me."

"You were too young to recognize it when it started. I don't think they would have treated us like they did Chad. I think guilt and fear over him stopped them from threatening to put us out. I managed to hold it together until I could get out of high school but I couldn't take it anymore. By that time you were already the favorite child and I really didn't care."

"I wasn't the favorite!"

"Okay, maybe favorite isn't the right word. The more dutiful. I knew I needed to get away and it seemed like it was too late for you."

"So you just left and let me spend years being their doormat. Why didn't you say something sooner?" China couldn't keep the anger and disappointment from surfacing.

"Would you have listened?"

"I guess not," China said thoughtfully.

Kelsey place her hand over hers for a second before she removed it. "Still, maybe I should have tried harder to make you see it. I'm sorry. So what has changed now?"

"I met someone and took him to their house for dinner."

"As in a man? Someone special?" Kelsey asked with a smile.

"Yes. A man. He told me he couldn't believe how I acted around them. That I shouldn't let them treat me the way they do. We had a big fight."

"Well, I hate to say it, but he's right. It's time for you to stand up to them. Stop letting them manipulate you. You don't have to please them anymore. You only have to please yourself. So tell me about this guy."

China blinked to keep the moisture from forming in her eyes. "There's not much to tell. We broke up. He's gone home."

"Home?"

"Chicago."

"Was he just here on vacation?"

"No, he was a doctor at the clinic. We fought and we haven't spoken since. He's not in town anymore."

Kelsey reached across the table and touched her hand. China looked at their clasped hands. It was the most sisterly thing Kelsey had done since she'd climbed into bed with her the night of the big fight between Chad and their parents. "So call him. Don't let our screwed-up family hurt your chance for happiness. Call him, find him, talk to him."

"I don't think he wants to have anything to do with me. He was so disappointed in me."

"Forget that. He'll get over it. Talk to him. If he cares about you he'll understand."

China squeezed Kelsey's hand. "Thanks for helping me see a few things clearer. I love you, sis."

Kelsey eyes glistened. "I love you too."

As they finished their tea they talked about Kelsey's

new job at the hospital. Finally China felt like she had her sister back.

Standing on the sidewalk in front of Kelsey's car, China said, "Thank you for coming. I wish we could do this more often."

"I'm glad I came also."

"Can we get together again soon?"

Kelsey took a while to answer. "I'd like that. But no pushing me to see Mom and Dad."

"I promise. This'll be about us. I've missed you."

Kelsey stepped over and hugged her. "I've missed my big sis too." She let China go. "Now, go call that fellow and tell him you've come to your senses."

"I'll think about it."

"We have enough regrets in our lives. Don't add another."

China watched as Kelsey got into her car and drove away. Would Payton listen?

She had lived in fear of being rejected, of not being good enough. Had Payton ever made her feel that way? No. She'd managed to twist what he'd said to her about her parents. Hadn't he proved more than once he wasn't like that? They'd worked together with patients, bought plants for his house and cooked dinner together, and never once had he ever criticized or talked down to her. He'd done nothing but make her feel good about herself.

She was such an idiot. When she'd spoken to him at the clinic it hadn't been about her, it had been about how he felt. She would think about what she needed to do later. Now, she was due at the clinic.

Once again she looked for Payton to show up for work. She listened for his footfalls in the hall and heard nothing. Sitting behind the front desk, she scrolled through the lab work that had come in to see if any of the patients needed to be called for a return visit or updated on the results.

She scanned the numbers of each patient, looking for any abnormalities. Her finger pushed the "scroll up button when the white cell count of a CBC was too high. This patient would need to be notified. Checking the left-hand corner of the page, the name of the patient jumped out at her like a flashing neon sign—Payton Jenkins.

China sucked in a breath. Her heart beat faster. Payton's high white cell count could be an indicator that his cancer was back. Had that been what the phone call had been about? Or did he even know? She had to tell him. Had to talk to him. See if he was okay.

Weak-kneed, she walked to the doctor's office and closed the door. More than once she'd had to make a confidential phone call from there. No one would question the door being closed and disturb her. With a shaking hand she reached into the pocket of her scrubs and pulled out her cell phone. Scrolling down until Payton's number appeared, she touched the screen.

Would he answer when her ID came up on his phone? Would he be glad to hear from her? The phone rang and rang and rang. With each ring her disappointment grew. His voice telling whoever was calling to leave a message came over the phone. She slumped against the desk. His voice, oh, how she loved the sound of Payton's voice.

At the beep, she said, "Payton, it's China. Your bloodwork came through. You need to call the clinic." Even to her own ears the message sounded cool and official. Nothing like one lover speaking to the other. But they were no longer lovers.

Her phone rang seconds later. Her heart leaped. She dropped the mobile. Was it Payton? Would he be as glad to hear her voice as she would be to hear his? With a shaking hand it took two tries to pick the phone up off the floor. The knot in her chest eased. The ID read "Mom." She touched the screen. "Hello."

"Hi, honey. Could you stop by and pick up a few things on your way over this evening?"

"Mom, I'm not coming."

"Honey, why not?"

"Mom, I'm not going to be coming over for some time. Also, please don't call me during work hours anymore."

"China, what's wrong?"

"I just need to make some changes in my life."

"You know your father is going to expect those pork chops of yours."

"You can fix them, Mom. There's some in the freezer. I've got to go now. Bye." China ended the call.

It hadn't been easy and she would owe her mom more of an explanation later but she had made her first move toward pulling away from her parents. Now she had to move forward and create a life without Payton. With her sister in her corner and her new understanding of herself, she felt empowered to do just that.

Payton looked at the blinking light on his phone. He'd missed an incoming call. *China.*

He ached for her with every fiber of his being. His fingers itched to touch her silky skin, kiss her full lips, hear the soft sound of her breathing next to him in the middle of the night. Things had already been difficult between them before he'd received the news from John about his questionable lab work. Emotionally he'd run, and he had no doubt she recognized it. Now all he wanted to do was repair the relationship, have China back in his life—permanently.

Just days earlier he'd caught the first flight out for Chicago and had been back in the hospital, undergoing tests, that afternoon. The flight had given him much-needed time to think, and the reality that he might be sick again, this time possibly worse than before, had made him re-evaluate China's words, "Life is about enjoying where you are, the simple things." She'd taught him that lesson well. Watching a storm, planting a flower and seeing it flourish or just spending time floating on his boat, and most of all making love to someone you cared deeply for.

He'd been running from life just as she had accused him of doing. That had led him to Golden Shores in the beginning but now he knew without a doubt that was where he belonged, especially with China. It was time to stop and face his monsters. Try to make his parents understand. Was his relationship with them any less dysfunctional than China's was with hers?

In its own way, no. He'd deal with whatever problem he had physically then speak to his parents in the hope he could get them to understand. No matter how that conversation went, he would have made the effort to offer the proverbial olive branch. That was all he could do.

Even if cancer had returned, he wanted China in his corner, helping him fight. And she would, if he hadn't hurt her so completely that she refused to have anything to do with him. That he might never make love to China again worried him more than what his tests might reveal. As the wheels of the plane touched down at O'Hare airport, he had his plan in place and the resolve to see it through.

Later that afternoon Payton pulled out his phone as he waited to have an MRI. He had to let his mom know he was in town. She would expect him to stay with her and his father. Payton would agree to stay with them, more in order not to hurt his mom's feelings than from need. When he'd spoken to John earlier that morning to let him know he'd be coming in, John had offered him a place to stay at his home.

Payton touched his mom's number and waited through the rings until her familiar voice came on the line.

"Hi, honey. It's nice to hear from you."

"You too, Mom. I just wanted to let you know I'm in Chicago."

"You are? Why didn't you let us know you were coming?" She paused then asked in a rush, "Are you coming home?"

She would think he was moving back but his home was now Golden Shores and China. "No, I'm here for some tests."

"I thought you weren't to have them until next month."

"My white count was high and John wanted me to come up for a look-see. I'm at the hospital now."

"Why didn't you call me sooner? I'm on my way."

Payton leaned forward in the waiting-room chair and propped an elbow on a knee. "No. I'm fine. Please, don't come to the hospital. I'll see you later this evening."

"I'll be there in a few minutes."

"Mom." He used a firm tone. "Do not come here. I appreciate your concern but I'm just having tests done. I won't know anything until tomorrow or the next day."

"I still think—"

"I know you care and I love you for that, but it's time we do it my way."

Her huff of resignation came over the phone. "You'll be staying here, won't you?" It was less a question and more a statement.

"Yes, if you'll have me."

"I'll be waiting. Your father will be glad to see you too."

Payton wasn't as sure about that. "Nothing has changed. I'll be returning to Golden Shores."

"I know, honey. I know."

Payton hung up. For once he'd managed to get his mom to back down. She'd taken his requests far better than he'd expected.

A step toward real change. Not the hyperstimulating changes he'd sought when he'd moved south but the solid, life-altering ones that brought true happiness. China had improved his world. Guilt washed over him. Instead of supporting her, he'd criticized her family, her life. His parents had certainly had expectations and aspirations for him. Payton could understand where China was coming from. He'd dumped on her about her relationship with her parents when his hadn't been much healthier. Making it up to her was going to take more than flowers.

That evening the taxi circled the drive of his parents' home and stopped in front of the door. Before Payton could finish paying the driver, his mom was on her way down the steps.

"Hi, honey," she said, with a bright smile, but her eyes carried the worry he'd seen so many times during his battle with cancer.

He wrapped her in his arms. She and China were a similar size. What was the saying? "Marry someone like dear old Mom." Marry! Did he want to marry China? He smiled. Yes, he did, if he could convince her to have him.

"So how are you doing?" his mom asked, studying him closely.

"I feel fine. Never better, actually."

"I have to admit you do look wonderful. The tan, the smile on your face. Living in Golden Shores looks like it agrees with you."

"It does." He wrapped an arm around her shoulders and led her toward the house. "Why don't we go see what Ruth has planned for dinner and I'll tell you all about it."

"I think there may be more than sand and sunshine to talk about."

Payton hugged her to him. "Mom, you know me too well."

Dinner was a formal affair, nothing like the spirited ones that he and China had shared or even those around the picnic table behind the clinic. Changes had occurred in him that had nothing to do with living in a new house or learning new things. They went soul deep.

It had happened. Something he'd resisted. He was in love. He'd promised himself he wasn't going there again, then along came China. He'd not been running for her sake but his. Fearing he might get hurt, he'd turned into a coward where facing up to his feelings were concerned. He was no different than his parents not wanting life to change, but it had on so many levels.

His father was present but outside of surface-level conversation he had little to say. His mom carried the conversation by asking about his new house, Golden Shores and the clinic. When she specifically asked about the people he worked with he told her about everyone, including China.

"You like this China, don't you?" she asked.

He should have known that his mom would pick up on the inflection in his voice when he spoke of China.

"So you've found a local." His father made it sound like Payton was hanging out with criminals.

"Yes, and I intend to marry her, if she'll have me." That thought brought a warm feeling in his chest.

"She's from a good family?" his mom offered.

"Mom, don't you want me to have a wife I love and who loves me, instead of just someone with the right pedigree?"

His mom didn't have time to respond before his father said, "Your position at the hospital is still open."

Payton pushed back from the table. "Dad, I know you were hurt and disappointed by my decision to leave the hospital and move to Golden Shores. I can appreciate that. I made a drastic change, shocked you and Mom. I realize that. I don't think I would have made such a decision if I hadn't already been unhappy with the direction my life was headed. I was going through the motions. Janice leaving me when I needed her most shows that I wasn't making solid choices. I never wanted to be on the board of the hospital. What I wanted and what I still want is to help people and be happy. I've found that in Golden Shores."

"But you had a good position. A chance to make a difference here," his father said.

"I still have all of that in Golden Shores, plus time to sail, enjoy the beach and cook for friends."

His father huffed.

"You don't have to like my choices, and that's fine. I would just like you to respect that they are mine to make. I would like you to be a part of my life and hopefully my family's life. Having cancer did change my outlook on how I want to live. That I can't deny. I just want different things now and I'm sorry that they're not what you had planned."

"You weren't happy here?" his father asked in little less than a growl of disgust.

"Not like I am now. I hope you can come to terms with that. If you can't, I'm sorry."

During the rest of his stay things were cool between him and his parents. He'd done what he could to get them to understand, now it was up to them to decide what they wanted from the relationship. He hoped for the best but would accept what they decided.

Crossing the Bay Bridge into Golden Shores brought him back to the present. He had to get China to listen to him. His first instinct was to drive straight to her place but she probably wouldn't even allow him inside. He needed to think. On the water was where he could do that best.

"China, there's a man on the phone who wants to speak to you," Doris called from the front of the building as China was stepping out of the employee entrance. It had been the longest week of her life and all she wanted to do was to go home and try to get some sleep.

With a sigh she turned around and walked back up the hall. Reaching the desk, she asked Doris, "Who is it?"

"I think he said Pete."

Pete. She didn't know a Pete, yet the name sounded familiar.

China picked up the phone, "This is China. How can I help you?"

"This's old Pete. You were with the doc when he got the hook out of my finger, weren't ya?"

"Yes, I remember you."

"I can't find the doc and me finger is the size of a net buoy, and all red."

Great. The man had an infection. Would at least need an antibiotic. It had been over a week, almost two. It should have healed by now but that dirty boat... "You need to go to the emergency room. The clinic is closed now."

"I don't have the cash. Already can't pay the bill from last time. Can you come by and give it a look? I can't find the doc."

A stab of pain hit in the area of her heart. She didn't know where Payton was either. "You're going to need medicine for the infection. I can't give you that. You're going to have to go to the hospital."

"I can't do that. Sorry I bothered you." He hung up.

China placed the receiver in the phone cradle.

"What was that all about?" Doris asked.

"Just a fisherman with a hook in his finger."

Doris twisted up her face. "Ooh. That doesn't sound like fun."

"It wasn't." *But Payton had been wonderful.* "I'll see you the day after tomorrow."

China only made it as far as the car before she'd made up her mind to go to the marina and check on Pete. She'd worry about him until she saw the finger for herself. All the memories of the time she and Payton had spent on his sailboat came flooding back as she turned into the parking lot of the marina. The urge to circle around and leave filled her but she couldn't let Pete possibly lose a finger or worse.

She pulled out the emergency bag she kept in the trunk of the car and started down the long pier. Passing where she thought she remembered Pete and Ralph's boat being moored, she kept walking. Her feet faltered. Soon she would be passing Payton's boat. Squaring her chin, she planned to walk by it without looking but at the last second she couldn't help but do so.

Her heart thumped against her ribs and her knees went weak. She stopped short. The bag slipped from her hands to plunk against the wooden boards beneath her feet. The stern of the boat faced her and printed on the transom in large, gold script letters was "*China Doll*." Payton had said that people named their boats after someone they loved.

A man stepped off what looked like Pete and Ralph's boat further down the pier. He stood silhouetted against the sunset. That physique she would know anywhere. *Payton.*

He started toward her.

Her stomach fluttered. "Uh, Payton, I didn't expect to see you." She glanced toward Peter and Ralph's boat but saw neither man. "Pete called and said something was wrong with his finger."

Payton stopped within touching distance.

She glanced at the boat. "Why?" she finally got passed the lump in her throat.

He said in a solemn voice with a tone of conviction, "Because I love you."

She stared at him. He looked wonderful, better than that, perfect. All she wanted to do was throw herself into his arms but she had her self-respect.

"China, you're starting to make me nervous. Say something."

"I have to check on Pete's finger." She made to move past him.

Payton caught her hand, stopping her. "Pete's finger is

fine. I asked him to call you. I didn't think you would talk to me so I thought maybe if I got you out here—"

"You could soften me up." She glared up at him. "You knew I'd come when Pete called, didn't you?"

"Yes. You have a soft heart. That's one of the many things I love about you."

She made a sound of annoyance in her throat. "How dare you talk to me about love. I don't even know where you've been for the last week. I saw your lab work. I've been worried sick. You just left. Someone who loves you doesn't do that."

Payton pulled her into his arms and brought his mouth to hers, effectively halting her tirade. His heart swelled when her arms slipped around his neck and she opened to greet him. She wouldn't make it easy on him but at least she wasn't immune to him.

He wanted her, had to have her, but on the pier wasn't the place. Payton broke the kiss but not the desire-filled fog China had wrapped around him. "We need to go aboard."

She looked at him with wide and dreamy eyes as if she'd forgotten everything but their kiss. He need to get her aboard before she came back to reality, which she would with a vengeance, he had no doubt. He wanted her relaxed and willing to listen when he explained.

Guiding China toward the boat, he let her go just long enough to hop onto the deck and then help her aboard. She came willingly. It wasn't until the clapping and wolf-whistling from the direction of Pete and Ralph's boat filled the air that she jerked out of her daze.

Payton swore under his breath. He pulled her close and dipped his head to distract her. She pulled away. It wasn't going to work this time. He would be paying the piper first. The talking would come before any lovemaking. "Let's sit here."

China waited until he sat on the bench and then she took a spot out of touching distance.

"Okay, go ahead and let me have it. I know I deserve it," he said, waiting.

"I have things to say but first I need to know about you. How you are feeling? What about your lab work?"

Payton reached to take her hand, which lay on the seat, but she placed it in her lap. "I'm fine. I'm sorry that I scared you. I shouldn't have run off like I did or lied to you about the phone call you overheard. You deserved better than that."

"So you went to Chicago?"

"Yes. I got back this afternoon. John, my doctor, wanted to run some tests just to make sure no cancer had reappeared."

Fear filled her eyes, which reassured him that she cared.

He smiled. "I got a clean bill of health. Apparently I had a sinus infection. While I was there I spoke to my parents, more specifically to my father."

She turned toward him, bringing one leg up to rest on the bench. "How did that go?"

Encouraged by having her full attention, he said, "I told him that I was sorry that I couldn't be who he wanted me to be and that I wasn't going to move back to Chicago. That I would be staying here and hopefully marrying you."

China's startled intake of breath filled the space between them.

"I told my parents that they'd have to accept that I had changed. They could be a part of my life or not, it was their choice."

She touched his arm briefly then removed it.

Skin that had suddenly been summer warm was abruptly winter cold.

"That had to have been hard to say."

"It was, but it needed to be done. And this needs to be

said also. I shouldn't have jumped on you about your relationship with your parents. Family dynamics are difficult enough, without someone who isn't a part of the family giving a commentary."

China wasn't sorry. "No, I'm glad you did. It made me see things I hadn't realized. I actually told my mom I wouldn't be cooking dinner the other day and said no when she asked me to go to the store for her. A small start but a start."

"I'm proud of you."

His words of praise added to the joy of seeing him. "I had tea with my sister too. I asked her about how I acted around my parents to see if you were right. She said she'd seen it for years. It was one of the reasons she had stayed away. She hated what they had and were doing to me. Best of all, she has agreed to start meeting me more often. It's the chance to get my sister back. I have you to thank for that."

He grinned. "Is there a possibility I might get a thank-you kiss out of that?"

"Not yet. I'm still mad at you. You tricked me into coming down here."

Payton looked contrite but not repentant. "Yeah, I didn't think you'd see me if I came to your place and I sure didn't want to have this discussion in front of the three musketeers at the clinic."

"Hi, Doc. I see she showed up. Looked like she wasn't so mad at you a while ago," Pete said with a huge smile from the dock. Ralph was standing beside him with an equally large smirk on his face.

China jolted at the sound of Pete's voice and looked away in embarrassment.

Payton chuckled. "Yeah, she did seem happy to see me."

"Well, we'll let yoz get back to what yoz was doing."

The burly men chuckled like two teenage girls and walked off, slapping each other on the backs.

Payton looked at China as the two men left. "Let's go for a twilight sail. We could use some privacy."

Half an hour later Payton had maneuvered them out into the middle of the bay and turned off the engine. While he dropped anchor China took a seat on the bench and placed her hands in her lap. Payton gave her a curious look as he passed her. Did he recognize how nervous she was? Seconds later the running lights came on, glowing red and green.

Payton returned to sit beside her.

"I like the new name for your boat," China said.

He smiled. "I was hoping you would. I'm a little cool. Would you mind moving closer and keeping me warm?"

China giggled. Payton always had a way of easing her jitters.

He laid his arm along the back of the bench, giving her an opening to accept. China waited a moment before she shifted over so he'd have to wonder if he'd gotten back into her good graces. She finally moved next to his big, warm body. His hand cupped her shoulder and pulled her in close but that was the only overture he made.

China was disappointed. She wanted to be kissed, made love to. She had missed him. After his passionate kiss on the pier she'd expected him to take her to the bunk the second the anchor hit the water. Instead, Payton had said he wanted to talk. She snuggled close and enjoyed being in his arms again. They sat quietly for a few minutes, looking off to the west at the pink and orange sky.

Payton broke the silence. "You know, if it wasn't for you teaching me to enjoy the simple things in life I'd have you in that cabin, taking your clothes off." His voice was calm and unhurried. He continued to look at the sunset. "I'm in love with you, China. If you'll have me, I'd like you to be my wife. I know it won't be easy. It will be years before I'm considered cured. I've treated you badly—"

China cupped his cheeks. "Shut up and kiss me!" She brought his lips down to hers. Her hands went to his waist and pushed at his shirt until she was forced to break the kiss so he could remove it.

"I thought you'd want to see the sunset," he murmured, as she slid down onto the deck and pulled him with her.

"I'm more interested in seeing you."

Payton gripped her shoulders, making her look at him. "Not until you answer my question."

China grinned. "I never heard a question."

"Okay, smarty pants. Will you marry me?"

"Under one condition."

He looked uncertain as he asked, "What's that?"

"That you never, ever leave again without telling me. I have to trust you to be here."

"I promise I will never leave you again by choice."

China sighed. That's all she needed. The security of knowing he would be there for her. "Then the answer is yes, yes, yes! I love you too."

Payton lay on the deck and brought her down over him. "Then how about showing me under the stars just how much."

China brought her mouth to his, waiting and warm.

A short while later the sun gave away to the black of night. China lay in Payton's arms on the deck, with a blanket beneath them and one thrown over them.

He nuzzled her neck. "I know you've heard of the mile-high club. Well, how about we start a new one? The mile-from-land club." He kissed the sensitive spot behind her ear.

China turned her head and found Payton's lips. "I'm more interested in being a member of the happily-ever-after club. With you, I will be."

* * * * *

Mills & Boon® Hardback
September 2014

ROMANCE

The Housekeeper's Awakening	Sharon Kendrick
More Precious than a Crown	Carol Marinelli
Captured by the Sheikh	Kate Hewitt
A Night in the Prince's Bed	Chantelle Shaw
Damaso Claims His Heir	Annie West
Changing Constantinou's Game	Jennifer Hayward
The Ultimate Revenge	Victoria Parker
Tycoon's Temptation	Trish Morey
The Party Dare	Anne Oliver
Sleeping with the Soldier	Charlotte Phillips
All's Fair in Lust & War	Amber Page
Dressed to Thrill	Bella Frances
Interview with a Tycoon	Cara Colter
Her Boss by Arrangement	Teresa Carpenter
In Her Rival's Arms	Alison Roberts
Frozen Heart, Melting Kiss	Ellie Darkins
After One Forbidden Night...	Amber McKenzie
Dr Perfect on Her Doorstep	Lucy Clark

MEDICAL

A Secret Shared...	Marion Lennox
Flirting with the Doc of Her Dreams	Janice Lynn
The Doctor Who Made Her Love Again	Susan Carlisle
The Maverick Who Ruled Her Heart	Susan Carlisle

0814GEN STD HB

Mills & Boon® Large Print

September 2014

ROMANCE

HISTORICAL

MEDICAL

Mills & Boon® Hardback
October 2014

ROMANCE

An Heiress for His Empire	Lucy Monroe
His for a Price	Caitlin Crews
Commanded by the Sheikh	Kate Hewitt
The Valquez Bride	Melanie Milburne
The Uncompromising Italian	Cathy Williams
Prince Hafiz's Only Vice	Susanna Carr
A Deal Before the Altar	Rachael Thomas
Rival's Challenge	Abby Green
The Party Starts at Midnight	Lucy King
Your Bed or Mine?	Joss Wood
Turning the Good Girl Bad	Avril Tremayne
Breaking the Bro Code	Stefanie London
The Billionaire in Disguise	Soraya Lane
The Unexpected Honeymoon	Barbara Wallace
A Princess by Christmas	Jennifer Faye
His Reluctant Cinderella	Jessica Gilmore
One More Night with Her Desert Prince...	Jennifer Taylor
From Fling to Forever	Avril Tremayne

MEDICAL

It Started with No Strings...	Kate Hardy
Flirting with Dr Off-Limits	Robin Gianna
Dare She Date Again?	Amy Ruttan
The Surgeon's Christmas Wish	Annie O'Neil

ROMANCE

Ravelli's Defiant Bride	Lynne Graham
When Da Silva Breaks the Rules	Abby Green
The Heartbreaker Prince	Kim Lawrence
The Man She Can't Forget	Maggie Cox
A Question of Honour	Kate Walker
What the Greek Can't Resist	Maya Blake
An Heir to Bind Them	Dani Collins
Becoming the Prince's Wife	Rebecca Winters
Nine Months to Change His Life	Marion Lennox
Taming Her Italian Boss	Fiona Harper
Summer with the Millionaire	Jessica Gilmore

HISTORICAL

Scars of Betrayal	Sophia James
Scandal's Virgin	Louise Allen
An Ideal Companion	Anne Ashley
Surrender to the Viking	Joanna Fulford
No Place for an Angel	Gail Whitiker

MEDICAL

200 Harley Street: Surgeon in a Tux	Carol Marinelli
200 Harley Street: Girl from the Red Carpet	Scarlet Wilson
Flirting with the Socialite Doc	Melanie Milburne
His Diamond Like No Other	Lucy Clark
The Last Temptation of Dr Dalton	Robin Gianna
Resisting Her Rebel Hero	Lucy Ryder

MILLS & BOON®

Why shop at millsandboon.co.uk?

Each year, thousands of romance readers find their perfect read at millsandboon.co.uk. That's because we're passionate about bringing you the very best romantic fiction. Here are some of the advantages of shopping at www.millsandboon.co.uk:

* **Get new books first**—you'll be able to buy your favourite books one month before they hit the shops

* **Get exclusive discounts**—you'll also be able to buy our specially created monthly collections, with up to 50% off the RRP

* **Find your favourite authors**—latest news, interviews and new releases for all your favourite authors and series on our website, plus ideas for what to try next

* **Join in**—once you've bought your favourite books, don't forget to register with us to rate, review and join in the discussions

Visit **www.millsandboon.co.uk**
for all this and more today!